HARPS FOR A WANTED GUN

Cy Harper, a youngster in search of a job, rides across the infamous desert known as Satan's Lair toward the isolated town of Apache Pass. As he reaches the midway point of the perilous ocean of sand, rifle bullets start to rain down on him. Mistaking Harper for a hired gunman known as Lightning Luke Cooper, more than a dozen unknown riders chase his high-shouldered black stallion for hours and keep firing. Finally, one of their bullets catches him. Is this the end for the innocent drifter?

TY WALKER

HARPS FOR A WANTED GUN

Complete and Unabridged

LINFORD
Leicester

First published in Great Britain in 2016 by
Robert Hale
an imprint of The Crowood Press
Wiltshire

First Linford Edition
published 2019
by arrangement with
The Crowood Press
Wiltshire

A catalogue record for this book is available
from the British Library.

ISBN 978–1–4448–4078–0

Published by
F. A. Thorpe (Publishing)
Anstey, Leicestershire

Set by Words & Graphics Ltd.
Anstey, Leicestershire
Printed and bound in Great Britain by
T. J. International Ltd., Padstow, Cornwall

This book is printed on acid-free paper

Dedicated with love to 'Ocean' Sue.

Prologue

The rapidly expanding Wild West was filled with every breed of wanted man. The majority of them had prices on their heads and were wanted either dead or alive. Most of these men were deadly killers, some were bank robbers. A handful of the more adventurous among them had perfected the art of robbing trains of their precious cargoes. To the bounty hunters who earned their blood money by hunting them down like dogs it did not matter which crime was committed: the reward money was exactly the same.

Not all wanted men were outlaws however, as the young Cy Harper soon found to his cost. The innocent drifter, like so many other young men after the war, had returned home to find that the very way of life he had fought for so gallantly no longer existed. Having nothing left apart from his thorough-bred black stallion and six-shooter, he headed deeper into the West in search of something most of his contemporaries would never find again.

He had travelled nearly a hundred miles and had reached a place called Satan's Lair. He was beginning to doubt the wisdom of his attempt to cross this barren desert when suddenly, out of the blue, rifle shots crackled in the still air.

Bullets rained down upon the innocent rider shortly after sunup. It took every scrap of his skill as a horseman to avoid the lethal lead. Harper whipped the rump of his large mount with the ends of his long reins and tried to outrun his attackers.

For more than twelve hours the youngster avoided the deadly shots that continued to seek his life. The black stallion had made good progress at the start of the chase but as the sun began to set the young man realized that his horse was flagging.

At last, after hours of ducking every shot that was fired at him, the young war veteran knew that he had to check his flight and start shooting back at them.

Harper rode over the crest of a parched ridge, reined in and dropped from his saddle. He watched as his mount trotted behind the cover of a nearby boulder. He drew his trusty .45 from its holster and took refuge behind another boulder.

The war had soured Harper's appetite for killing. He had stopped keeping count of the men he had wounded or killed after the first battle. It had become a sickening bloodbath, setting brother against brother. After a few months of waging war the youngster had no idea why any of them were fighting.

The gun felt heavy in his hand as he stared out into the sun-baked desert. It was the first time he had held the weapon at the ready since the war had ended.

Reluctantly he cocked the gun hammer until it locked into position. He waited. The dying rays of the setting sun cast a strange reddish light across the desert. It seemed as though the arid land was starting to bleed.

Harper had lost sight of his followers behind a high bluff five minutes earlier but he knew they were still trailing him from the sound that only a lot of saddle horses could make.

Then he spotted them. His eyes widened in shock.

This was the first time he had remained stationary long enough to see how many riders were hunting him down. There were far more of them than he had imagined.

The setting sun lit up the approaching horsemen as they spurred after the tracks of their prey. As the last rays of the sun danced across their rifle barrels it appeared as though they were emerging from Hell itself.

Who were they? he silently wondered.

Why were they hunting him?

Although Cy Harper was not a wanted outlaw he knew that here were more than a dozen gunmen who thought differently. For some reason they were determined to kill him. They wanted him dead.

He had to fight back. There was no other option. It was either fight or die.

Harper crawled around the side of the boulder and wished that he owned a rifle like those of his pursuers. His six-gun did not have the range to engage them on level terms.

He knew that he would have to let them ride even closer than they already were if he was to have a chance of hitting any of them. Memories of the war returned to his tired mind.

He aimed his Colt at them through the shimmering heat haze.

They kept coming. They were like a phalanx of impending death, but Harper had faced far worse odds in his time during the war. When the conflict had ended he had vowed never to shoot anyone again, but that was now a promise that it was impossible to keep.

They wanted him dead. Would he ever discover why?

The setting sun was in their eyes. That was a slim advantage; Harper was going to take full advantage of it.

Then he wondered: what if they were the law?

Sweat trickled down his face.

Whatever they were, they had been trying to kill him for twelve hours now and Harper was tired of running.

Carefully he took aim.

As they came within range Harper squeezed on his trigger. A deafening bolt of fiery venom spewed from his six-shooter and cut a path through the darkening distance between him and his pursuers.

His aim was as true as it had been on the battlefield. One of the riders raised his arms and tumbled backwards off his horse. Before the horseman hit the ground, Harper had cocked and fired his gun once more.

Harper continued to fire again and again until his gun was empty. He scrambled to the other side of the smooth rock and reloaded. He quickly turned and frantically fired at the riders. He had to stop them, he kept telling himself.

Another of the horsemen released his grip on his reins and went flying over his saddle cantle. Dust rose around the horsemen as they reined their mounts to a halt. The desert resounded with the noise of Winchesters being cocked.

Suddenly their rifles blasted at him. The side of the boulder was hit by at least a dozen shots. A similar number of shots passed above the crouching Harper's head.

The innocent drifter had been forced to fight back but it did not sit well with him as he continued to squeeze the trigger of his six-shooter.

After a while the air was filled with acrid gun-smoke. Cy knew that if the riflemen had their way they would send him to meet his Maker. He had no intention of joining the heavenly choir just yet.

During a brief lull in the gunplay Harper fired one more shot into the middle of the gunsmoke. Then he turned and slid down the sandy slope to his horse.

He ran through the twilight and leapt up on to his high-shouldered stallion. He poked his boots into the stirrups and spurred.

The stallion raced across the desert sand. Harper hung on to his reins and holstered his smoking gun as the mighty stallion tore away from the scene of the brutal fight.

It did not take long for the riflemen to realize that their prey had fled. Within seconds they opened up again with their rifles. Shots flew after him as Harper encouraged the stallion to even greater speed.

The powerful animal charged through everything in its path in its attempt to escape the fearsome bullets.

Harper felt the heat of the lead as it

flew all around him like a swarm of crazed hornets. The air was filled with the stench of gunsmoke. The young horseman knew that his trusty mount needed water, food and rest or it would not last much longer but there had been no time. Somehow the black stallion was still finding the strength to obey him. For how long would it be able to keep doing so? he wondered.

The stallion jumped down into a gully and powerfully forged on across the flat desert. Harper clung on to his long leathers as shots tried to claim his hide. He did not mind the sound of gunplay. It meant that he was still alive.

As Harper cleared a rise he again caught a brief glimpse of the remaining horsemen charging after him. There were still at least a dozen of them in hot pursuit. White flashes lit up the darkening sand as they fired their rifles again.

Harper was not a wanted outlaw but they wanted him.

They wanted him dead.

Ducking beneath the hot tapers of death the young drifter gritted his teeth and urged his exhausted mount on in defiance of the rifle shots that streaked after him. This was not going to be easy, Harper thought, as his hands gripped his reins.

The rising moon in a cloudless sky illuminated every feature in the landscape. Harper drove the black stallion on across the vast desert in search of cover; he knew that one mistake would be his last. He could hear their hoofs drumming behind him. As even more shots cut through the eerie moonlight, Harper held himself low over the stallion's head. One bullet hit his canteen and nearly ripped it free of his saddle horn. It spun on its long leathers for a few moments before the youngster saw the gaping hole it its side.

He looked back and drew his six-gun. He fired at his pursuers, then rammed the smoking weapon back in its holster. As the mighty horse maintained its mile-eating stride Harper reached down and lifted the canteen. It was dry.

A terrifying realization flashed through his exhausted mind. Even if he found water in this parched desert, he no longer had anything to put it in.

Harper tossed the useless vessel away in angry frustration.

The relentless sound of pounding hoofs grew louder and clearer. Was one of the riders gaining on Harper's now flagging black stallion? He glanced over his shoulder again. He was right: one of the riflemen had broken away from the others, leaving them to eat his dust.

The lone horseman was rapidly closing the distance between Harper and himself.

Harper turned and watched in horror as the rider raised his rifle and aimed it at him. It seemed a fair bet that once he had squeezed the Winchester's trigger the only sound Harper would hear was that of angelic harps.

1

Only a few hours before Cy Harper stopped his impressive black mount in a hopeless attempt to fend off the riflemen, the owner of another black stallion had been making his way through those very streets of Long Horn City where the youngster had walked hours earlier.

Unlike the innocent Cy Harper, this man was infamous for his merciless gun skills, his forte being the robbing of some of the largest banks in the territory.

However, Lightning Luke Cooper had been unlucky this time, for no matter how hard he tried he was unable to find a weakness in the settlement's bank. The premises were virtually impregnable and it seemed his journey had been in vain — until he made his daily visit to the telegraph office.

The message he received there offered him a chance of making some blood money. He fanned his chin with the scrap of paper and grinned to himself as he proceeded down the main street.

Fate had once again saved his blushes and presented Cooper with a way to make the long ride to Long Horn City profitable after all. Cooper had always been able to hire out his gun skills to whoever met his price, for there was always someone ready to pay hard cash to the notorious outlaw. Most men would have to work for an entire year to earn the fee that Cooper could get for simply putting a deadly accurate bullet into someone.

His cruel eyes darted around the busy street. He chuckled to himself as he watched the townsfolk going about their daily rituals. Cooper despised them and would not think twice about slaughtering any or all of them if called upon to do so.

Long Horn City was situated on the

very edge of the harsh terrain that the locals called Satan's Lair. The arid desert beckoned only the brave or the foolhardy, for if there were waterholes in its arid wastes only a very few people knew of their existence. Yet some men dared to test themselves and their mounts and ride across the vast expanse of sand and rock in order to reach the distant towns.

Some paid the ultimate price for their defiance of Nature. Satan's Lair was covered with the bleached bones of those who had not made it. But regardless of the dangers and for various reasons men still chose to make the treacherous ride.

The only man-made objects to be seen along the trail were wooden poles with telegraph wires strung between them. Setting up the telegraph connection had been a costly affair; more than thirty-six men had died from various causes while setting up the link across the desert.

Long Horn City gave no visible clue

to what lay just a few miles west of its unremarkable streets of red-brick and wooden buildings. But the town had prospered where others had simply become ghostly memories.

The solidly constructed bank was set in the very centre of the sprawling settlement, a financial stronghold that was the envy of all of its counterparts in other towns. The bank was built of steel, red brick and concrete. Some said it was impregnable; others tried to devise a way of breaking in to its reinforced vault.

The bank was favoured by most of the cattle ranchers along the western side of the territory and their fortunes were deposited in its safes.

That was why the infamous Lightning Luke Cooper had been drawn to Long Horn like a moth to a flame. Yet even Cooper, who had arrived in Long Horn a few days earlier, could not find any weakness in the bank's defences.

The wanted man read the telegram again. A mirthless smile played across his hardened features. Cooper would charge top dollar to his would-be paymaster. He would make sure that he would be recompensed for not being able to rob the fortress-like bank. The trip to Long Horn City would prove profitable after all, he vowed.

Although most folks had heard of the notorious outlaw, few ever recognized him. As a man with a price upon his head he had always been careful to remain in the shadows.

The name of Lightning Luke Cooper was worth big bounty but, unlike many of his fellow wanted outlaws, he had never had a photographic likeness taken. Not even an artist's sketch adorned his Wanted poster.

That meant that Cooper had been able to walk freely around Long Horn as he vainly tried to work out how to rob the bank. Almost no one had given him a second glance as he picked up a request for his blood-spilling talents at the telegraph office. Even those few who did recognize him gave no sign of it, for fear of his reputed mercilessness.

Lightning Luke held the telegram in his hand as he strode down the main street of Long Horn. It was from someone he had worked for previously. A man whom he had once wronged but who now seemed to have buried the hatchet and was in need of his deadly services again.

Cooper gave an evil grin and slid the scrap of paper into his pocket.

Someone was doomed to die. That was the only reason anyone ever sent for Cooper. He would happily kill anyone if his fee was met.

He stepped off the boardwalk and made his way through the busy traffic towards the livery. A drunken cowboy staggered from a saloon and stepped between Cooper and the weather-worn stables. The cowboy, staring at the man with guns hanging from his hips, raised his hand until it was level with Lightning Luke's chest.

Lightning Luke Cooper stopped in his tracks and looked at the cowboy angrily. There was fury in his eyes at being prevented from advancing.

'What you want, cowboy?' he drawled in a cold icy tone.

The drunken cowboy grinned at the deadly gunman.

'Ain't I seen you before, dude?'

Cooper rested the palms of his hands on his gun grips and looked the rangy cowboy up and down. He nodded his head and spat.

'I reckon you must have,' he answered. His thumbs flicked the safety loops off his gun hammers. 'The trick is I don't give a damn. Get out of my way or I'll kill you.'

Fuelled by liquor the cowboy stepped forward.

'Who do you think you're talking at, dude?' he growled. 'I ain't scared of no stinking outlaw like the famous Lightning Luke.'

With no expression on his face, Cooper drew one of his .45s faster than the cowpuncher had ever seen anyone draw a gun. Cooper pushed the gun's barrel up against the cowboy's throat and forced his challenger back. The startled cowboy only stopped backing up when his spine collided with a brick wall. Lightning Luke pushed the cold steel forcefully against the young man's windpipe.

'Now you give me a good reason why I don't have to pull on my trigger, partner,' Cooper growled menacingly. The cowboy blinked hard.

'What kinda reason?' he croaked.

Cooper lowered the six-shooter. Then, faster than a lightning bolt, he slashed its barrel across the side of the cowboy's head. The youth toppled sideways and crashed on to the boardwalk. A pool of blood gathered around his cracked skull but he was still alive.

The wanted outlaw then took hold of the cowboy's bandanna and dragged his stunned victim into the depths of an alley. He released his grip and stood staring at the crumpled heap at his feet.

The cowboy rolled on to an elbow

and peered through the blood pouring down his face.

'You are Lightning Luke?' he squeaked in a terrified whisper.

Cooper drew one of his matched six-shooters again and nodded at the dazed cowboy.

'Yep, I'm Lightning Luke OK. Now go tell the angels that I killed you.'

Before the cowboy could utter another word Cooper again smashed the barrel of the gun on to his head. He repeated the action forcefully several times until there was little left that was recognizable of the cowboy's skull apart from a hideous crimson pulp. The gunman grinned, cleaned the .45 with his victim's bandanna, then holstered the gun. He turned and walked on to the livery.

Lightning Luke entered the cool livery stable and wordlessly nodded at the blacksmith. The heavily muscled man knew what Cooper wanted without needing to enter into conversation. He led the tall black stallion out of its stall and began to saddle it for its infamous owner.

Lightning Luke Cooper watched silently with ice-cold eyes as the burly blacksmith prepared his prized mount for the long ride to Apache Pass.

Even though Cooper had always been careful not to allow his image to be taken, so as never to be recognizable, he had overlooked one thing: the like of his handsome black stallion was rarely to be found in this part of the country. Anyone seen riding such a creature could almost certainly be no other than the lethal Lightning Luke Cooper.

The magnificent animal was his Achilles' heel. It was the one identifiable aspect of Cooper that bounty hunters knew about: he always rode a distinctive black stallion.

'Fill two extra canteens for me,' Cooper demanded as he paced around the large livery.

'Sure thing.' The blacksmith did as instructed. He plucked two brand-new canteens off a peg near his forge and filled them with cold water from his water pump. He hung them from the stallion's saddle horn and wiped his huge hands down his leather apron.

Quietly he led the stallion across the earthen floor towards the silent Lightning Luke Cooper.

'It's a pleasure looking after a fine stallion like this 'un,' he remarked. 'This boy got breeding.'

Cooper tossed a golden eagle into the blacksmith's hands and took the long leathers from him. He led the horse to the large open doors, then paused.

'You sure got yourself a mighty fine horse there, stranger,' the blacksmith went on, patting the animal's hindquarters.

'There ain't another one like him in the whole of the territory,' Cooper drawled as he checked his sidearms. The blacksmith shook his head.

'You're wrong.'

Lightning Luke narrowed his eyes.

'What you mean?' he growled in seeming disbelief.

The blacksmith rubbed his hands over his sweat-soaked face and sighed heavily. He looked at the frowning outlaw.

'There's another black stallion just like this 'un in the territory right now,' he explained. 'His young rider rode on out of here in the early hours. He was headed for Apache Pass.'

Cooper rubbed his jawline. 'He was riding a horse like mine? Are you sure?'

'Yep, and the young loco-bean was headed across the desert.' The blacksmith sighed. 'They'll both be bleached bones in a couple of weeks. Satan's Lair ain't no place for anyone to try and cross this time of year.'

Cooper raised an eyebrow.

'Is that right?'

'Yep. That desert don't take prisoners.'

Lightning Luke Cooper was thoughtful for a moment. He wondered who would be riding a black stallion as fine as his in these parts.

'Where you headed, stranger?' the

liveryman asked.

Cooper stepped into his stirrup and hoisted himself up on to the back of the stallion. He looked down at his questioner.

'Apache Pass,' he replied. He withdrew a cigar from a pocket and bit off the end. 'I got me a job to do over there.'

'You ain't figuring on trying to cross Satan's Lair, are you?' the blacksmith asked.

Cooper glanced down at the big man. 'I sure am.'

'But that place is deadly.'

'So am I,' Lightning Luke drawled. 'So am I.' He placed the cigar between his teeth

The blacksmith surveyed the guns strapped to Cooper's hips and the Winchester resting in its scabbard under the saddle leather. He backed away as Cooper drove his spurs into the tall stallion's flanks and rode out towards the desert known as Satan's Lair.

24

The sweat-stained liveryman did not know it but he had just spoken to Lightning Luke Cooper. He watched as the rider steered the stallion towards the desert. He sighed.

'Reckon the buzzards are gonna get themselves another free feed,' the big man muttered. He shook his head and strode back into the livery.

2

Dust swirled up into the star-filled sky as nightfall gradually got the better of another blistering day. The heavens had yet to turn black but with every lash of the rider's long leathers the darkness deepened. Cy Harper glanced heavenwards briefly and cursed the cloudless sky and the bright moon. A moon which would frustrate his every effort to escape the bushwhackers.

The rider who had broken away from the pack was now within twenty feet of his stallion's long tail. So far Harper's horsemanship had enabled him to escape the venomous wrath of the rider's Winchester. He rose in his stirrups and looked back.

The rider, whoever he was, had the repeating rifle tucked into his shoulder and was aiming it at Harper's back. Suddenly a deafening report blasted out. The heat of the rifle bullet burned Harper's face.

Snorting like a raging bull, the powerful black stallion thundered down a draw. Then it responded to its master's commands and found new strength to gallop along the dry riverbed. Even so, Harper could not shake the rider off his trail. He looked back and watched as the horseman drew even closer.

Harper could see the metal barrel of his rifle glinting in the moonlight. Then he heard the sound of its hammer falling upon an empty magazine.

His rifle was out of lead, Harper told himself. He dragged back on his reins and stopped the exhausted stallion in its tracks. He turned and leapt at his pursuer as his charging horse passed within inches of him. Harper caught the rifleman around the chest with his outstretched arms. Both riders tumbled from their mounts and hit the sand hard.

It was Harper who got to his feet

first. He threw a left and a right fist into his winded opponent's jaw. Then he grabbed at the man's bandanna, pulled it towards him and unleashed a final right cross.

He staggered back to his foe's mount and snatched a canteen from the unconscious man's saddle horn. He could hear the rest of the riders approaching quickly.

Harper threw his aching body on to the back of his black stallion, hung the canteen on the saddle horn and spurred his horse into action.

Harper knew that he was killing his prized mount but there was nothing else he could do. There was no option but to keep running and praying for salvation. He knew that every one of the riders behind them would kill him given a chance.

The strange twilight created a million monsters all around the devilish terrain, but even his imagination could not create anything as frightening as the danger from which he fled. He looked back over his shoulder for the umpteenth time and saw their rising dust in the moonlight.

His mount climbed up a sandy slope.

Upon reaching the level top of the rise the horseman dragged back on his reins and steadied the snorting animal. The horse pawed at the sand as its master rubbed the grime from his eyes. With dust floating around the stationary horse, the rider stood in his stirrups and looked across the starlit land behind him.

He dismounted, filled the bowl of his hat with water and watched as his horse drank every drop of the precious liquid. Harper took a gulp from the canteen then screwed the stopper back on to its neck. He hung it back on the saddle horn, then snatched up his hat from the sand where it had fallen.

Harper gripped his long leathers and mounted the tall black horse again. He gathered the reins in his hands and looked around the vast unholy terrain that surrounded him.

The telegraph poles and their long lines sparkled in the frosty air. Harper reasoned that if he followed the direction of the wires he would eventually find Apache Pass.

He slapped the stallion's rump and steered the spent animal towards the telegraph poles. Terror gripped his heart as his mind still tried to explain why the mounted riflemen had turned their weaponry on him and chased him for so long. Harper simply could not fathom what their motive could be.

Unless, he reasoned, they had mistaken him for somebody else. Mistaken him for a wanted outlaw. They looked like a posse; maybe that's what they were. A posse determined to kill their prey and share the reward money. A cold shudder traced his backbone.

Was that why they just would not quit chasing him?

Harper allowed the stallion to find its own pace as it cut along a dry riverbed and he listened to the sound of their horses' hoofs growing louder. On reaching a thicket the tired youngster eased back on his reins and allowed the stallion to rest for a few moments.

He stared around him with dust-filled eyes. He could no longer see the telegraph poles but knew roughly where they were. It was the sound of the riflemen that filled him with dread.

He patted the lathered-up neck of the stallion and prayed that the water he had given the thirsty animal might enable them to escape the bullets of their foes.

Twelve hours ago it had seemed doubtful that he would keep them at bay for more than a few minutes. Now it felt like a miracle that they still had not overwhelmed him.

Harper knew that he was living on borrowed time.

A thousand unanswered questions flashed through his desperate mind as he steadied the huge horse and continued to search the ever-darkening arid land. The desert offered little in the way of cover and Harper knew it. He had to find some place that he might call sanctuary, though.

He dropped down to the sand again and poured the last of the canteen's contents into his upturned hat. Again he held it under the stallion's grateful nose. As the horse drank, Harper again pondered the situation he found himself in.

Had they mistaken him for a wanted outlaw? Were they a posse hell bent on claiming the bounty they thought they would earn by killing him?

Was that it?

Was it that simple?

The horse finished drinking and Harper replaced the hat on his head. The drops of water felt good against his aching head and burning skin.

He continued to stare out into the darkness. There was still no sign of them, he thought. Not yet. They were close though. The sound of the horses relentlessly trailing him echoed all around him.

He gripped his saddle horn and

hoisted his weary frame up on to the back of the high-shouldered animal. He hung the empty canteen against the stallion's flank and tugged the reins to his side.

The stallion slowly walked up the rise from the riverbed until it was back on level ground. Then Harper's heart skipped a beat as he looked back and saw the raised flickering torches of the men who hunted him.

Cy Harper watched their fiery torches against the backdrop of the distant mountains that fringed the desert.

They were still coming, he thought.

Harper looked all around the ever darkening desert in the vain hope of seeing something that might offer him cover. But wherever he cast his thirty-year-old eyes there seemed to be nothing but sand.

He lifted himself up, balanced in his stirrups and stared ahead. The eerie moonlit desert still shimmered as the cold night air dragged the last of the heat from the sand.

It was like looking into a dizzying whirlpool.

Nothing seemed as it should.

He knew he could not trust anything in this unholy terrain to be what it seemed to be. Harper sat down in the saddle again and tried to think.

His burning eyes stared through the moonlight at the torches. They were held high in the hands of the horsemen, who were closing the distance between themselves and their prey with every beat of his pounding heart.

'Damn it all!' Harper cursed in bewilderment. 'Don't them bastards ever quit?'

Now, with their torches, they were following the distinct tracks left by his horse's hoofs.

No matter how hard the weary horseman tried, he could not imagine any other resolution to his situation than his ultimate death. Harper was no stranger to facing the blazing guns of his enemies after two long years in the cavalry during the war, but this was different.

Very different.

The guns of enemies fighting for a cause was one thing, but to be shot at and hunted like a prize stag was something else. It seemed to Harper that there was no way out of this situation other than continuing to run for his life.

Yet his horse was spent and Harper was equally exhausted. The drifter did not know how much further he could ride before the magnificent black stallion folded beneath him.

Harper checked his Peacemaker. He had thinned out their ranks but that gave him no pleasure. He had thought his killing days were behind him; he had been wrong.

It seemed that sometimes the only thing that will stop men from killing is to kill them first. A cold shiver ran down his spine. As he slid fresh bullets into his gun's chambers he knew that the imminence of death would never allow him to forget the taste of killing.

It was now a choice of fighting or dying.

Neither choice sat well with Harper. He tried to swallow but there was no spittle in his tinder-dry mouth. He tapped his spurs, urging the stallion to take a few paces forward as his gaze darted back and forth.

Then he noticed a dark patch against the horizon. His eyes squinted hard as they tried to work out what he was looking at. The stallion continued to walk slowly on as its master strained his eyes in an attempt to fathom what the dark patch might actually be.

'Trees?' Harper exclaimed. 'Is that trees?'

He steadied his spent mount.

Then the desert shook as thunderous rifle shots carved through the night air and passed all around his broad shoulders. Harper looked back in stunned shock at the horsemen. They were now approaching him much faster than before.

As more shots exploded from their weapons Harper stared at the plumes of gunsmoke that encircled them. Red-hot tapers of light whizzed close to the magnificent stallion.

Harper swung round on his saddle and spurred. The horse jolted into action and started to flee from the deathly bullets.

'Who in tarnation are those guys, Jet?' he growled angrily as once again he lay low over the neck of his valiant horse. 'I'll get us out of this pickle somehow.'

The black horse defied its exhaustion and kept galloping into the eerie twilight as the sound of bullets echoed around the barren desert.

Harper desperately sought sanctuary. He needed to take cover behind a big boulder or an old adobe wall, but the desert did not seem to have any such features.

Harper screwed up his eyes and stared at the dark patch ahead of his charging horse. What could it be? It might be a wall or remnants of an old adobe, he told himself. Whatever it was it was getting closer with every stride of his mount's long legs. Could he at last have found the one thing he needed to conceal him from his hunters?

His eyes narrowed as they strained to see into the eerie gloom. Rifle shots rang out behind him. Harper looked back at the horsemen.

It was as though the Devil's henchmen were bearing down upon him. Harper knew his snorting mount was close to dropping but he had to keep urging it on.

'Whoever them varmints are,' he snarled wearily, 'they'll not quit until they bury me. I sure wish I knew why.'

He dragged the reins to his left. He was about to spur again when he felt the heat of more bullets passing within inches of his face. He slapped the loose ends of his reins across the stallion's rump.

The gunfire sounded like distant thunder. The venomous shots were instantly upon him. The bullets whizzed all around him like crazed fireflies. The smell of burning air filled his flared nostrils as he tried to steady the large black stallion.

Then just as Harper managed to get the skittish mount under control he felt a violent thud in his left shoulder. He arched in agony as the bullet which had entered his back burst out from just under his collarbone. A spray of scarlet gore showered over the horse's dark mane.

For a few paces the young horseman was barely able to stay astride his mount. His shaking hands grappled with his loose reins until he managed to regain control of the horse beneath his bloodstained saddle.

Somehow the stallion did not miss a stride.

Harper gripped the saddle horn with one hand as with the other he lashed the ends of his long leathers across the flowing mane of the stallion.

'Keep going, Jet boy,' he urged as

exhaustion threatened to overcome him. 'Try to reach cover.'

A pain unlike anything he had never experienced before tormented his swaying body. His clouded eyes glanced up to look at what lay ahead of them; the sight that greeted them filled him with astonishment.

They were approaching a grove of trees growing just beyond the edge of the arid desert sands. He summoned up his last drop of strength, cracked the leathers at the ground and wearily urged the stallion on.

Even though he was racked by the agonizing wound, Harper knew that if he could just reach the trees he might find the cover he desperately sought.

'Try to reach them trees, boy,' he managed to yell at his lathered-up horse. 'Try your best, Jet. Just try and reach them giant toothpicks and maybe we'll live a tad longer.'

The stallion continued to move far faster than should have seemed possible. It thundered across the pristine sand despite its exhaustion. Then its head bucked up unexpectedly. Harper realized that the animal had caught the scent of something.

The stallion flared its nostrils.

'What can you smell, Jet?' he asked as his horse produced another burst of speed. Whatever the black stallion had detected, it was obviously something it craved.

Fighting unconsciousness Harper suddenly realized that there was only one scent that could so energize an exhausted horse: the brave stallion could smell water.

The shots were still ringing out behind him but the wounded young rider no longer cared. His dust-caked eyes tried to focus on the trees as his valiant mount approached them. He slumped on his saddle and hung on as the stallion carried him over a moonlit crest and down the other side. Their followers' bullets hit the sand, showering both horse and rider in fine granules.

What Harper had espied from the desert was only the tops of the tall trees: now he realized that they were far bigger than he had first thought. He clung on as his mount, the smell of fresh water filling its nostrils, kept on sliding down the loose gravel towards the beckoning trees.

Harper was drifting in and out of a deep sleep. Death wanted Harper but he was not ready to die just yet.

The stallion reached the bottom of the slope and continued to keep moving to where its instincts guided it.

Harper's eyes cleared temporarily. The sight of the leafy branches of the trees roused his weary mind. As he tried to steady himself atop his saddle he caught sight of the wet stain down his shirt front. The bluish moonlight filtering through the trees' canopy made the blood gleam.

Harper felt like a rag doll as blood flowed freely from his chest. He swayed helplessly in the saddle as the stallion swiftly weaved its way between the trees, avoiding every obstacle as it made for the water that it sensed was close by. All Harper could do was slump on its high shoulders as he drifted in and out of consciousness.

Every fibre of his being wanted to submit to the sleep that he craved but Harper knew that only death lay that way. He had to try to stay awake. Nearly falling from his saddle, Harper brought the stallion to an abrupt halt. For a few moments he tried to regain control of his mind. A swirling mist confused his thoughts as he rubbed his eyes and tried to make sense of where he was. The mighty thoroughbred pulled at the reins as the smell of fresh water filled its nostrils and only its insistent jerking kept the young drifter awake as he held the stallion in check.

'Easy, Jet,' he mumbled.

Harper cast his fog-filled eyes all around him at the countless trees. Nothing seemed to make any sense.

He had fought many battles in his short life but none of them had been like this. Terrifying memories tormented his drifting thoughts as he fought desperately to outwit the Grim Reaper. He blinked hard but it was like staring into a mirage.

His eyes were lying to him. He no longer knew if what he was looking at was real or just another figment of his confused brain.

He pushed his pointed boots further into his stirrups and braced himself to avoid falling from the saddle. His shaking hands fumbled with his long leathers until he had the stallion on a short rein. Death was whispering into his ear but Harper refused the temptation to listen to its soothing promises.

He was just about to let the snorting stallion start moving again when a barrage of shots lit up the trees. The black horse reared up and kicked out at the devilish streaks of light.

Harper could see the gunsmoke. The riders were firing their rifles but luckily the tree trunks absorbed the bullets. However the deafening noise had achieved one thing. They had startled Harper out of the delirium which had been killing him.

Feverishly Harper lifted the tails of his reins and whipped them across his mount's shoulders. The courageous horse leapt into action and thundered its way into the depths of the woodland.

Bullets ricocheted off the trees as the galloping stallion thundered through the labyrinth of woodland. The scent of precious water was drawing the large horse onwards like a magnet. There was nothing Harper could do except hang on for dear life.

The headstrong stallion twisted and turned among the trees and under-growth in its quest for the elusive water. Gradually Harper noticed that the shooting had stopped. Pain was racking his entire body. He leaned over the saddle horn, allowing the stallion to find its own pace. All he could do was try and ensure that he was not thrown from the horse's high shoulders.

It took all of his dwindling strength

just to hold on to the frantic stallion as it leapt over every obstacle in its path. It was like trying to slow down a runaway freight train. Somehow the few moments of rest had renewed the stallion's boundless energies.

The dazed horseman realized that the darkness was deepening as he rode further into the wood. The eerie moonlight could no longer penetrate the leafy density of overhanging branches. Summoning every last drop of his failing energy Harper hung on to his reins as the muscular horse pressed on towards the tantalizing scent of water.

At last even Harper could smell the nearby water. He leaned back and gave a sigh of relief. But then, as the stallion turned sharply, a low-hanging branch caught the young drifter cruelly across his bloodstained chest.

Harper was winded. The force of the blow lifted him off his saddle and over the cantle. All he knew was that he was no longer astride the large stallion, he was somewhere else. Harper was flying helplessly backwards through the darkness.

He hit the ground hard. Then he realized that he was still moving: he was being tossed about alongside the pounding hoofs of the stallion.

His right boot and spur were entangled in the stirrup leather. Harper was being dragged through the rough undergrowth of the thicket by the black stallion.

Desperately he tried to free his boot but it was impossible. After a few yards Harper lost his battle to disentangle himself and was knocked senseless.

The wide-eyed stallion continued to run on into the depths of the wood, seeking the precious water it craved, with its unfortunate master still in tow.

3

Judge Rolf Brewster raised his hand
and stopped the riders as they reached
the spot where one of their bullets had
hit Harper. The full moon cast its unholy
illumination down on to the sand and
made the unmistakeable droplets of blood
sparkle like discarded diamonds.

Brewster glared at the dark trees
some way beyond the riders, then he
studied the sand. A cruel smile
stretched across his harsh features.
From their vantage point the wooded
land appeared in total contrast to
Satan's Lair. The tall trees were so
densely packed together that none of
Brewster's hired guns relished the idea
of chasing anyone into their midst.

But it was not the trees that had
chiefly caught the judge's attention, it
was the sand just before his mount's
hoofs.

The self-proclaimed judge stared down at the glinting gore, then looked at his small army of riders. He gave a nod of his head.

'What you seen, Judge?' Red Farrow asked as he heard their leader grunting with amusement.

'Don't any of you see it?' Brewster pointed at the sand and gave a satisfied chuckle. He lowered his large frame from his saddle and waved the flaming torch over the churned-up sand. 'Our friend Lightning Luke Cooper seems to have started leaking blood, boys.'

The rest of the horsemen looked down at the sand where Brewster indicated, then they all nodded.

'We finally plugged that slick bastard, Judge,' Dan Peters said, grinning in agreement as his eyes saw the moonlit trail of glistening gore. 'A blind man could follow the trail he's left.'

Brewster handed his torch to one of the riders and moved to his horse's shoulder.

'Yep, you plugged him OK. By the looks of it he's bleeding real bad, boys. By my estimation he'll be dead before sunrise.'

Lane Brown held his rifle across his midriff and looked down at the judge. He alone was not convinced that they were chasing the outlaw they had been hunting for more than half a day. He pushed the brim of his sweat-soaked hat off his brow and looked down at Brewster.

'How can you be so damn sure that's Lightning Luke's blood down there, Judge?' he queried. 'We must have bin a quarter-mile away from that varmint when you ordered us to start shooting. Even a bald eagle might have had trouble seeing him clearly.'

Brewster darted his gaze at Brown.

'Who else would it be, Lane? It was Lightning Luke OK. I recognized that big black stallion of his. Can't be more than one big black thoroughbred in this territory and it belongs to Lightning Luke Cooper. Savvy?'

Brown nodded respectfully. 'I savvy, Judge.'

'That horse of his must be worth a pretty penny, Judge,' Dan Peters opined. 'When we get our hands on it I reckon we should draw straws to see who owns that stallion.'

Judge Brewster stared up at Peters.

'I'll own it, Dan. It'll be mine unless you've got any objections.'

Peters shook his head.

'I ain't got any objections, Judge,' he murmured.

'Good,' Brewster said with a snarl. 'I'd hate to have to kill you for getting greedy, Dan.'

The riders were sore and tired. They had been waiting to ambush Cooper for hours before the rider of the black stallion had crossed their path.

'When do you figure we'll catch up with Lightning Luke, Judge?' Vince Dolby wondered. He placed a twisted cigarette in the corner of his mouth and struck a match. He cupped its flame and then sucked smoke into his lungs.

'I don't know about the rest of the boys but I'm plumb tuckered.'

Brewster nodded and stared across the sandy expanse. His keen eyes were picking out the trail left by the blood their quarry had lost in his flight.

'I'm sore just like the rest of you, boys,' he admitted. 'But we'll find Cooper's dead carcass in the next couple of miles. Nobody can lose that much blood and live for long.'

A satisfied grunt ran along the line of horsemen.

Farrow slowly dismounted and held the bridle of his weary mount as he inspected the animal.

'We'd best water and grain the horses, Judge,' he advised. 'They're in bad shape and no mistake.'

Judge Brewster nodded firmly. 'Red's right. Water and feed the horses and let them rest for a while. There ain't no rush any longer. When we catch up with Lightning Luke, he'll be dead.'

Every one of his hired gunmen dismounted and did as the judge ordered. The horses were in bad shape after their long chase.

Judge Brewster took hold of his reins and nodded at his dusty entourage. The cruel grin returned to his face.

'All we gotta do is follow his tracks. Nobody can bleed the way he's bleeding for too long and live,' he said. With his long fingers he pulled a cigar from his jacket pocket and placed it between his teeth.

Peters bit his lip thoughtfully.

'How'd you know Lightning Luke would be headed across the desert, Judge?' he asked.

'Because I sent for him, Dan,' Brewster replied. He snorted as he ignited a match with his thumbnail and set its flame to the end of the long dark weed.

Looking confused, Peters emptied the contents of a feed bag on to the sand for his mount.

'You sent for him?' he repeated. 'And then you had us wait to bushwhack the critter. How come?'

The judge stared towards thicket of trees, which showed darkly in the eerie light, and exhaled a line of grey smoke. He then looked at his inquisitive hireling.

'Lightning Luke Cooper is worth a tidy sum dead or alive, Dan,' he stated. He removed the cigar from between his teeth and stared at its glowing ash. 'I figured it was time I claimed the bounty on his head. I wired him to come to Apache Pass to earn big bucks. He never could ignore the prospect of money.'

Dolby stared at their leader. 'I thought Lightning was a pal of yours, Judge.'

'He was until he wronged me, Vince.' Brewster sighed heavily. 'There was a time when I figured we were best of friends but he wronged me. Now it's his time to pay. Nobody wrongs me.'

'I guess not,' Dolby said, shrugging his shoulders. Brown looked across at the judge.

'How much did you say this critter is worth, Judge?'

'Fifteen thousand bucks, boys,' Brewster answered. Again that cruel grin creased his features

The line of riders chorused a grunt of excited satisfaction. They were like a pack of starved hounds with the scent of a fox filling their noses.

'That's a mighty big heap of money,' Farrow observed. Brewster roared with laughter.

'I told him I had a sweet little job for him to do for me. I just failed to tell him that it meant him dying.'

The riders laughed. The ominous sound echoed across the moonlit sand.

Brewster turned to face his dishevelled riders. He glared at them and then back at the trees down in the glade below them.

'Take the saddles off the horses,' he commanded. 'Rub these nags down. We've got plenty of time, unlike poor old Lightning. We'll rest up for a while and then go looking for a dead man.'

'How'd you know where he'll head, Judge?' Brown asked. 'A wounded varmint ain't likely to think clearly.'

Brewster sat down and savoured his cigar.

'Even a wounded Lightning Luke will head to Apache Pass 'coz there ain't no other place in these parts for a critter to get himself some doctoring,' he answered.

Vince Dolby edged closer to Brewster and looked down at the smiling older man.

'What exactly did Lightning Luke do to wrong you, Judge?' he asked.

Judge Brewster shot him a glance.

'If I told you that I'd have to kill you as well, Vince boy,' he replied coldly. 'Now tend to my horse and quit being so curious.'

4

The coal oil lights of Long Horn City shone like beacons in the darkness of the night. They lured not only a multitude of insects to their glowing lanterns, but something far more deadly. No one had seen the stealthy approach of the horseman as he and his mount led his packhorse through the darkness towards the outskirts of the sprawling settlement. Yet the scent of death hung in the air around the body he had draped over the back of his pack animal.

The horseman raised his scarred countenance and stared with half-dead eyes at the town ahead of them. A wry smile crept across his unshaven features as he guided his mount into the outskirts of the busy town.

Mort Dooley straightened up and pulled one of his six-shooters from its holster. His dust-caked mount continued to respond to the bloodstained spurs that kept jabbing it in its scarred flesh.

The bounty hunter had earned a good living over the previous five years, having dared to do what the law was either unable or unwilling to attempt. He had risked his hide to bring in wanted outlaws for the price on their heads.

To date he had slain eleven of the West's most notorious and valuable of badmen and was not finished yet. The merciless bounty hunter had received information that one of the most elusive outlaws was in Long Horn City. Even though it had meant bringing his latest victim fifty miles out of his way, Dooley had decided to follow the scent.

The tall horse walked slowly on its long legs into the main street as its master glanced around for any hint of trouble. Men like Dooley did not last too long if they forgot to treat everyone as a potential assassin.

Two lanterns set at either side of a door drew the deadly hunter of men towards the sheriff's office. Light from within the small brick building glimmered around the edges of its drawn blinds and spilled out on to the boardwalk. Dooley eased back on his reins and looked around at the faces of the town's people. The sight of his scarred features was as effective as his arsenal of guns at keeping them at bay.

Dooley swung his long right leg over the cantle of his saddle and eased his muscular frame down. As he hitched his long leathers to the pole he continued to listen to the awe-inspired chatter his appearance had evoked.

The bounty hunter untied the packhorse and led it to stand beside his mount. He secured its reins to the pole, then walked around the animal to inspect the decaying remains of the dead outlaw roped to its back. The rotting body filled the street with its sickening stench.

Dooley rested one hand against the

body on the packhorse and curled his fingers round his gun's trigger. He raised his .45 up into the air, cocked its hammer and fired the weapon. The deafening sound echoed up and down the long street.

It did not take long for the door of the office to open. The sheriff burst out with a scattergun in his hands. The lawman looked startled as he caught sight of the bounty hunter, just in time to see Dooley holstering his weapon.

Sheriff Walt Stone stepped out on to the boardwalk and was suddenly hit by the fetid stench of the rotting corpse. He covered his nose and mouth with his hand and stared at the tall bounty hunter.

'What in tarnation are you up to, boy?' the sheriff snarled, keeping his double-barrelled shotgun trained on the bounty hunter.

Dooley walked towards the wary sheriff. He stopped just short of the boardwalk and pushed his hat back on to the crown of his head.

'I'm Mort Dooley. I'm a bounty hunter, Sheriff,' he drawled. There was no sign of emotion on his hardened features. 'I brung in Ted Grundy for the reward money.'

Sheriff Stone fanned his face in a vain attempt to rid his nostrils of the sickening stench which made his head reel and agitated his guts.

'Hold on there a damn minute. There are ways to do this kinda thing, boy,' Stone riled. He backed up to his office door. 'You just don't ride into town and start shooting up the place in order to announce your damn arrival.'

'Why not?' Dooley asked. He rested a boot on the boardwalk and watched the lawman's every move. 'It got you out here, didn't it?'

Trying to hold his breath Stone stepped down and walked to the decaying outlaw. He used his shotgun's barrel to move the head of the corpse. His eyes squinted at the decomposing features.

'How'd I know this is Ted Grundy?'

he asked. 'This could be anyone.'

Angrily, Mort Dooley turned away from the boardwalk and marched to the lawman's side. He grabbed hold of the dead man's hair and shook it until the head came away from the body.

Dooley held the head in his grip and rammed it towards the startled sheriff's face. Stone gasped in horror, then turned and doubled over.

The bounty hunter waited for the lawman to finish spewing up before he continued to lay his claim.

'You satisfied? This is Ted Grundy, OK. I'll swear on the Good Book to that, Sheriff.'

Sheriff Stone staggered to a nearby water trough and pumped ice-cold water over his head until it was numbed. Then he straightened up and stared through the droplets of liquid at the big bounty hunter.

'OK. I'll agree that's G-Grundy,' he stammered. 'Now take it away and bury it.'

'He's worth a thousand dollars,

Sheriff,' Dooley growled. 'I want my money or I'll nail this to your porch.'

Stone rushed into his office and hastily scribbled on a scrap of paper. He returned and thrust the note into Dooley's free hand.

'Take this chit down to the Wells Fargo depot,' he said. 'They'll pay you.'

Dooley dropped the detached head and pulled a knife from his belt. Its honed edge cut through the rope that was securing the rest of the wanted outlaw's body to the pack animal. Dooley then dragged the body off his horse and watched as it crumpled into the sand.

'You best get the undertaker down here if you want this critter buried,' the bounty hunter said. He slid his knife back into his belt, then walked to the water trough and washed the slime from his hands.

Stone stared at the rotting pile of flesh and bone and then looked at the unconcerned bounty hunter. He was about to voice his anger again when

Dooley stepped to within inches of him and eyeballed the lawman.

'Where's Lightning Luke Cooper?' the bounty hunter unexpectedly asked. Stone raised his eyebrows.

'How should I know?'

Dooley grabbed Stone by his shirt front and lifted the lawman up on to his toes. His eyes burned into those of the lawman.

'I reckon you know,' he whispered. 'Cooper's got a way of frightening you star-packers. You figure it's best to look the other way when he's around. He's got a habit of killing folks and it's best if you pretend you ain't seen him. I'll ask you again, where is Lightning Luke Cooper, Sheriff?'

The lawman swallowed hard, then nodded his head in acquiescence. As he felt the bounty hunter's strong grip relax he lowered his wet head.

'You're right,' Stone admitted. 'Cooper was in town, but then he got a telegram. The operator told me that it was from Judge Brewster in Apache Pass. Cooper headed on out for Apache Pass as soon as he got the message.'

The bounty hunter rubbed his unshaven jaw thoughtfully.

'Is he still riding that big black stallion?' he asked.

Stone nodded. 'Yep. He's still riding that big horse.'

'Good.' Dooley plucked the scrap of paper from his pocket and looked at it. 'It makes it a whole heap easier to identify that varmint.'

'You're going after Lightning Luke?' Sheriff Stone gasped.

'Why'd you think I come so far out of my way, Sheriff?' Mort Dooley sighed heavily. 'First I'm going to get my bounty money for Grundy from Wells Fargo. If I was you I'd go wake the undertaker up and get him to plant that stinking outlaw. He's sure ripe enough.'

He turned and walked along the dusty street away from the trembling lawman.

★ ★ ★

Ice cold water lapped against Cy Harper's face, slowly awakening the young drifter from his deep slumber. Although Harper had been quite unaware of it his black stallion had dragged him for nearly a mile along the ground to Devil's Creek.

Harper's eyes opened and the bemused man stared up through the moonlight at his boot, which was still lodged in his stirrup. Harper slowly forced his aching body up from the shallow water and grabbed the fender. He tried to get his bearings but it was impossible.

Unlike the infamous Lightning Luke Cooper, he had never been this way before. Harper glanced around him at the water which had soaked through his torn trail gear to his skin and so had cleaned his wounds. He then glanced at his horse.

The black stallion was calm as it filled its belly with the sweet flowing water and plentiful grass. The animal did not move while its master gripped the fender to haul himself upright.

Mustering every scrap of his remaining strength Harper slowly managed to haul himself up until he was balanced on his free leg. The stallion still did not move. Harper then tried to free his entangled boot from the twisted stirrup.

After what felt like an eternity Harper managed to free his boot from the leather restraints and stand on two feet again. His gloved hands gripped the saddle while he rested his pounding head against its cold leather.

He was giddy and cold.

Harper exhaled loudly and stared over the brow of the saddle at the tall trees that grew beside the creek. He tried to figure out where he should head for now. Logic told him to go downstream. There were usually towns at the end of creeks, he told himself.

The filtered moonlight danced on the fast-moving water as slowly he recalled what had happened to him. His fingers instinctively touched the raw wound in his chest. The cold water that had lashed over the brutal wound had stopped its bleeding.

He tightened the string of his wet hat under his jaw and took hold of his saddle horn.

He touched the wound again. It felt like having a red-hot poker pushed right through his chest. The searing pain reminded him of the shot that had nearly killed him. He looked all about him but so far, it seemed, the riders had not located him.

'I gotta get moving before them critters show up again, Jet,' he mumbled to the stallion as his numb fingers tried to gather up his reins. Then another thought came into his dazed mind.

Although the freezing water had stopped the bleeding whilst he had been lying in the creek, Harper knew that unless he got the raw wounds tended to soon, it was only a matter of time before they began to spew gore again.

He gritted his teeth.

He defied his agony, gripped his saddle horn in his left hand, carefully raised his leg and poked his boot toe into the stirrup. He hoisted himself up and somehow he managed to swing his right leg across the stallion's broad back. He rammed his boot toe into its stirrup and gathered up the long leathers.

'I wonder how much blood you gotta spill before you're dead, Jet boy?' he mumbled, rubbing his still blurred eyes. 'I sure feel like I ain't got a whole lot left, and that's for sure.'

Harper had no idea how long he had been unconscious and therefore he did not know how close his pursuers were. They had tracked him for half a day and he knew that the trail of blood he had left before ending up here would bring them in on him like buzzards to a carcass.

Fearing that he had no more time to waste he pulled the head of the stallion up from the water and urged the powerful animal on.

The big horse started to move.

The leafy branches of the trees that fringed the banks of the creek gave him cover as he encouraged the big black horse to find more speed. Every stride that the big horse took was agony to Harper.

'I gotta find someplace to rest up,' he muttered as the stallion continued to pound its hoofs into the water. Spray rose up and glinted in the eerie moonlight as the bedraggled horseman hung on like a tenderfoot. 'Someplace where them riflemen can't find me.'

Harper narrowed his eyes and studied the winding route of the shallow creek ahead of him. Maybe there would be a settlement or town ahead where he might find help, he hopefully told himself. All he needed was a place where he could rest until he regained his strength and was able to fight back.

Flashes of heavenly light glanced through the canopy of branches both horse and rider as Harper kept tapping his boot heels against the stallion's flanks.

Cy Harper felt as if death had already visited him but somehow he had managed to escape the wrath of the Grim Reaper for a while.

Still, he knew that when death wanted you there was little anyone could do but resign himself to the inevitable. He was still dizzy from the loss of blood, but he gritted his teeth and fought his overwhelming desire to fall into a deep sleep.

That would be the sleep from which there was no awakening.

Harper shuddered.

As the mighty stallion gathered pace, the same haunting thought kept nagging at his tired brain: when would the riflemen reappear?

When would the shooting start again?

5

The light of a full moon and a myriad of stars gleamed down upon the small group of crude buildings that stood close by the bank of the shallow stream. The homestead was nestled amongst a scattering of trees and was barely noticeable from the waterway, which cut a course between the entangled brush and the big trees.

The door of a cabin opened and closed quickly as a woman dressed in a white nightgown came out into the large yard. The heavenly light made her freshly washed hair appear like the finest silk as it spread across her shoulders. She made her way stealthily towards the creek.

With every barefoot step she glanced fearfully back over her slender shoulder at the cabin. Each night she would slip out from her matrimonial bed for a few fleeting moments in a vain attempt to find something she had once believed a wedding ring would bestow upon her.

The gently flowing creek allowed her a few precious moments in which she could forget the harsh reality that fate had bestowed upon her. The rhythmic sound of its ankle-deep water had a calming effect upon the woman and allowed her to imagine things she was now resigned to never knowing in reality.

Every night she would stare at the creek as its water flowed past her and dream of the knight in shining armour who would end her torment and take her to a place where she would be happy and free.

But he never came.

Slowly she reluctantly had to admit to herself that she had exchanged one sort of prison for another. She had fled from the squalor of life in New York to the virtual slavery of a loveless marriage in the West.

Betsy had resigned herself to the

situation she had willingly entered into. There was no escape for a mail-order bride with no money. What little she had arrived with in Apache Pass was now a fleeting memory. Her only pair of shoes had worn out six months earlier and her other possessions had suffered the same fate.

Since her wedding day Betsy had only left the homestead when she was taken to the church in Apache Pass on Sundays. These were the only times when her husband allowed Betsy to venture away from the homestead.

Not even when her husband, Moses Applegate, had to go to town and get provisions did he allow her to accompany him. Like so many men of a certain age Moses was possessive. As far as he was concerned she was just another of his possessions: no more important than any of his livestock.

Betsy was twenty-six years old. Moses was at least twenty years her senior and cut from a much sterner cloth than his mail-order bride. For two long years she had done everything a wife is meant to do but she had never once felt even a smidgen of love from the drunken Bible-quoting pig farmer.

The cabin Applegate had built close to Devil's Creek was scarcely any better than the dwelling he had constructed for his prized hogs. Even the barn where he kept his fine pair of sturdy shires had been built with more care.

Like so many men in the West, Applegate had paid an agent and in turn accepted his wife with little more rejoicing than he had shown when he had paid hard cash for a new boar. Betsy Holmes had travelled with women in similar circumstances from the slums of New York to her new home, expecting a husband who would love her. Like the majority of her travelling companions she had been cruelly disappointed.

Moses Applegate had purchased himself a bride. He had married Betsy because he needed someone who could provide him with carnal satisfaction and who was young and strong enough to do some of the work that was becoming too much for his ageing body. It was as simple and heartless as that.

In effect he had purchased himself a slave.

Like most God-fearing women Betsy did as her husband wished without ever complaining, for no matter how bad her situation was, it was better than the one she had left in New York.

Yet as the still handsome young woman walked from the cabin towards the creek, which ran along the boundaries of her husband's pig farm, she still harboured the dreams which had made her travel halfway across the country. The dreams of being sent for by a young, strong man still burned into her romantic imaginings that were so unlike the reality which she had silently accepted.

Betsy still yearned for affection.

Betsy rested her shoulders against the moonlit tree trunk and sighed as the creek water lapped at the muddy bank. This was a nightly ritual which she had undertaken every evening after Moses had crawled into her bed and fallen asleep, having consumed untold quantities of hard liquor.

Each evening Betsy would lie on her back and succumb without ever complaining to whatever her drunken spouse demanded, for she had taken a vow to love, honour and obey. No matter how many indignities she endured, her marriage vows remained sacred to her.

Betsy would never break a promise sworn on the Good Book.

Moses's snoring was her signal to slip out of bed and go to spend a few precious moments alone. Betsy had dreamed of the man she had naively thought would be waiting for her at the stage depot in Apache Pass: her imagination had been fuelled by many dime novel stories. But when she saw the aged Moses Applegate for the first time her heart sank.

Within days the shocked Betsy had found herself married to Applegate. Only then did the reality of her situation dawn upon her. By that time it was too late.

Now, every night, as she strolled through the starlight in her long nightdress, the dreams of what might have been returned to her. Dreams of the handsome knight in shining armour who, she secretly prayed, might come to take her away from the hideous slavery in which she now found herself trapped.

Only her dreams kept her sane.

If nothing else, Betsy was still an optimist.

As her large beautiful eyes watched the glowing light of the moon trace across the quickly moving water, she heard an unfamiliar sound. Betsy stiffened and peered towards where the noise was coming from.

For two years she had heard every sound the creek could make; she did not recognize this sound. Then she realized what she was hearing. It was the sound of a horse's hoofs as it made its way through the water of the creek. She could hear it splashing in rhythmic steadiness.

Had her prayers somehow been heard and answered? Were the glorious imaginings of her deepest yearnings finally becoming a reality? Her heart pounded in silent hope.

Betsy lifted the hem of her nightdress and stepped closer to the water's edge. Her eyes stared through the gloom in excited anticipation. She felt her heart quicken: she had never been so excited. Her small hands cupped her face as, with her large beautiful eyes, she watched for what felt like an eternity for a glimpse of the approaching horseman.

Then she saw him.

Droplets of water sparkled in the moonlight as the horse drew closer to the spellbound Betsy. The black stallion looked far more powerful than any other horse she had ever seen as it rounded the bend and cantered towards her.

The rider was slumped over its head. No matter how hard Betsy tried she could not make out what he looked like, but there was something about him that set her pulses racing. The shafts of moonlight gave the horse and rider an almost ethereal appearance. Betsy felt warmth surge through her.

Suddenly she was racked with guilt. It washed over her like a tidal wave, although she had not done anything to warrant such an emotion. But Betsy felt as though somehow her prayers had been answered: prayers that no married woman of any decency should ever offer up.

Betsy glanced guiltily at the cabin, then back at the mysterious horseman. She pushed the loose strands of her hair off her face and composed herself. She placed her bare foot into the water and stepped into the shallow creek.

Betsy then raised her hands.

With no thought for her own safety

she waved frantically at the approaching horse in an attempt to stay its progress. The sight of the slim young woman in her nightgown spooked the large horse and it shied.

As beams of eerie moonlight played upon Betsy's long gown the horse slowed its pace. Only the sight of a ghost might have unnerved the stallion more. It snorted at the defiant figure. Betsy continued to wave her arms at the wide-eyed horse until it stopped in mid-stream. Only then did Harper glance up. He looked at Betsy's shapely form from under the brim of his Stetson with as much surprise as that shown by his horse. The moonlight was making her nightdress appear almost transparent and Harper rubbed his eyes, expecting to wipe away the beautiful vision he was staring at. Yet no matter how hard he rubbed, she remained there, standing in the icy-cold water.

'If I didn't know better I'd reckon I must have died and gone to Heaven, ma'am,' Harper said with a sigh as he held his nervous mount in check. 'You *are* an angel, ain't you?'

'I'm no angel.' Betsy threw caution to the winds and splashed through the water until she was standing next to the stallion's head. She looked up at Cy Harper's face and was lost in wonder at his handsome looks.

She caught her breath. It suddenly dawned on her that Harper appeared exactly as she had imagined her knight in shining armour would look.

There was just one exception: he was wounded.

'You're hurt. Are you OK?' Betsy asked. She moved along the horse's flank to take a closer look at Harper's leg. Wearily, Harper forced a smile.

'I'll be honest with you, ma'am. I've bin a whole lot better.'

'My name's Betsy,' she told him.

'They call me Cy.'

Betsy glanced towards the cabin and then back at the injured horseman. She did not know what to do next. For countless nights she had prayed for something like this to happen but now she was afraid. Then her keen eyes noticed the bullet hole in the front of Harper's shirt.

'Have you been shot?' she asked anxiously.

Harper tried to hide the evidence of the bullet that had passed clean through his body. His hand rested over the torn fabric of his shirt.

'I'm afraid so, ma'am,' Harper reluctantly replied. 'If I don't find myself somewhere to rest up, I reckon the varmints who are hunting me will finish me off.'

'Who's hunting you?' Betsy asked anxiously.

'I ain't figured that out,' Harper answered.

'Why are they trying to kill you?'

'I ain't figured that out either, Betsy.' Harper winced as pain ripped through his shoulder. 'They sure are determined though. I don't think they'll quit until I'm dead.'

A million questions flashed through Betsy's confused mind but before she could ask any of them Harper slumped forward again. His gloved hands gripped the saddle horn and sweat dripped from his forehead. It was clear to Betsy that the handsome young drifter was in agony and that it was all he could do just to remain in his saddle. Her small hand reached up and tenderly touched his arm.

'Don't worry. I'll take care of you. I'll fix up your wounds so they won't start bleeding again.'

For some reason he trusted her. Maybe it was because she looked like an angel in her long nightgown. It might have been because she was kind and braver than anyone he had ever encountered before. Whatever the reason, Cy Harper knew that she was exactly as she appeared. There were no false frills or graces about the young woman he knew only as Betsy.

He glanced down at her. He could not understand why she was showing him kindness but he surely appreciated it.

'Why would you risk helping me, ma'am?' he asked. 'It could be mighty dangerous for you. Those riflemen seem content to kill anything that gets in their gunsights. It'd be a whole lot safer for you if'n you just let me be.'

She frowned. 'I ain't your ma'am. My name's Betsy, Cy. Don't you recall me telling you? And if I wanna help you that's exactly what I'm gonna do. Savvy?'

'I savvy.' Harper touched the brim of his hat. 'I still reckon it might be dangerous, helping the likes of me, Betsy. I'd hate for any of them varmints to hurt you.'

Betsy waved a finger. 'You let me worry about that. You need looking after and that's what you're getting.'

Suddenly they looked directly at each other. For a moment neither said a word as they simply stared into one another's eyes in the grip of a strange emotion that neither of them had ever experienced before, or truly understood now. At last Betsy turned away from his searching gaze. She cleared her throat and pushed strands of her long hair off her face. Her small hand gripped the stallion's bridle as she led Cy's mount towards a gap in the trees.

Then an ominous noise drew their attention. Betsy looked around into the shadows as it grew louder. Harper raised his head and peered back along the creek. Then he cast his gaze down on Betsy. Moonlight illuminated her features.

'You hear them?' he asked.

Her eyes flashed as she nodded.

'Riders,' she whispered.

Harper glanced back. He could see the red torchlight flickering off the undergrowth and trees.

'They're coming again, ma'am,' he warned.

6

The oncoming horsemen appeared more akin to creatures from the underworld than to regular riders. The scarlet light from their raised torches lit up the trees and the branches hanging over the creek as Judge Brewster led his deadly followers through the shallow water. The beat of their horses' pounding hoofs grew louder with every passing minute.

It sounded like the rumbling of distant thunder but Betsy knew that it was something far more dangerous: the sound of many horses riding through the shallow water in search of their wounded quarry. The noise echoed around the thicket of trees, growing louder, seeming to accompany every beat of her racing heart. Harper straightened up in his saddle and looked over his shoulder. He swallowed hard.

'Damn it! They're closer than I figured,' he exclaimed. 'Reckon you'd better go, ma'am. They'll probably hurt you as well.'

'No they won't.' Betsy led the stallion to the narrow gap. 'They ain't gonna hurt either of us.'

The skittish black horse shied and refused to follow her up into the field beyond the trees. Harper kicked his heels into the stallion's flanks.

'Get moving, Jet,' he growled into the stubborn animal's ear. 'Follow the lady.'

Frantic, Betsy stared back at the torchlight. They would be rounding the bend at any moment, she thought. When they did, they would start shooting.

Without stopping to think any further Betsy hitched up her long nightgown with one hand and grabbed the stallion's bridle with the other. She gave an almighty tug that started the stallion walking again. The feisty young woman led the exhausted horse through the narrow gap. When Jet was safely in the field Betsy quickly piled loose brush against the gap in the trees.

'That should fool them back-shooting heathens,' Betsy growled. She took hold of the horse's bridle again, urged Jet to a trot and ran along beside him.

She led the way across the muddy soil towards the barn. After every few steps she looked back at the cabin, fearful that Moses might have woken up and found her missing.

Betsy had only just guided the tired horse into the barn when she heard the sound of the dozen or so riders kicking up water as, coming along the creek, they passed the now concealed gap in the trees.

She stopped, turned to the open barn door and looked in horror across the yard. The flames of scarlet light flickered amongst the trees as the line of horsemen rode on towards Apache Pass. Just like the wounded drifter behind her, she too wondered who they were.

Whatever the answer, they were a chilling sight; it would remain branded into her memory for as long as she lived.

Betsy cast her attention back to the young man she knew only as Cy. He had been right when he had told her of the hunters on his trail. She swallowed hard and bit her bottom lip as her mind raced.

There were many more of them than she had imagined.

Who were they and why were they intent on killing him? She looked at Harper, seated on the black stallion. He did not look dangerous or anything like the descriptions of outlaws she had read about in the many dime novels she had once so much enjoyed.

Why should they be trying to kill him?

Her eyes darted between the cabin, the trees and the young wounded man. Her heart was racing: she did not know which she feared most. Was she afraid of what the riflemen might do if they caught up with the young man? Or was it that she was terrified of what her husband might do if he found her in her nightdress with a stranger?

Maybe she feared most the emotions that the young wounded man was arousing deep inside her: emotions that were growing stronger with every passing moment.

She knew that she was wrong to feel like this, and yet it seemed so right.

Betsy glanced across the barn at her husband's pair of shire horses. Then she reached up and helped Harper to dismount. Although young, he was drained of strength. She wondered how much blood he must have lost before he reached this homestead. He looked like a ghost.

As his boots touched the earthen floor he gave a pitiful moan and fell away from her arms. He landed heavily on a pile of loose hay. Panic raced through her. She dropped to her knees beside him and brushed his face with her soft fingers.

'You better not be dead,' Betsy said, pressing her hand against his ice-cold forehead. She looked closely at his chest, trying to make out whether it was moving or not. In the dimly lit barn she could not tell.

Betsy dropped her head on to Cy Harper's damp shirt. Her long hair covered him as she pressed her ear against his chest. To her relief he was still breathing and his heart was pounding almost as rapidly as her own. He required help but she was unsure as to what she should do.

She had never felt so helpless.

Betsy bit her lip and rose to her feet. Every fibre of her knew that she had to help the young unfortunate man who lay at her bare feet.

But how?

Then the image of her brutally vicious husband Moses filled her thoughts again. She pressed her fingers to her trembling lips. Terror gripped her. Moses had used his belt on her many times in the previous two years for no better reason than that he could do it. It was as though he believed it was his duty to beat the Devil out of her at every opportunity. Betsy feared that finding the handsome young stranger with her in the barn would provoke him into an uncontrollable rage.

Moses Applegate got mighty righteous when fuelled by liquor, and tonight he had drained a jug dry before staggering to their bed.

Betsy cast her eyes down at Harper again. Suddenly, as though by magic, her dread of what her husband might do evaporated into thin air. Her head tilted as she looked down upon Harper's handsome face.

No knight had ever seemed so perfect, she thought.

Betsy had never seen a grown man look so vulnerable before. However much she feared the retribution her husband might inflict upon her, she had to help this handsome stranger.

She took a deep breath, unhooked his empty canteen from his saddle and walked to the water barrel in the corner of the barn. She filled the vessel and returned to Harper.

Without a second thought Betsy knelt beside Harper, raised his head up from the hay and nursed it next to her fluttering bosom. Carefully she put the canteen to his lips and poured water into his mouth.

At first the water just trickled down his face. Then to her relief he responded and started to drink the liquid he had craved for so long.

Betsy smiled as his eyes flickered and opened. A tear of joy ran down her cheek.

'Feeling better?'

'What happened, ma'am?' he asked, and sighed as his tired eyes focused on his Good Samaritan. Even the darkness could not hide her beauty from him.

'You passed out.'

Harper looked embarrassed. 'I've bin doing that a lot since I tangled with them bushwhackers.'

'Them shooting you might have

something to do with it, Cy.' She pushed his hair off his forehead and studied him more clearly. Every nerve in her body urged her to kiss him but she knew that would be wrong. 'I thought you were dead there for a minute. I was real scared.'

'I ain't dead.' He sighed. 'I hurt too bad to be dead.'

Betsy rose to her feet and walked towards the barn door. She glanced back at him as he lay on the straw. She smiled.

'I'll sneak back here with some vittles in a while,' she told him. 'Then I'll sew up your wounds.'

Harper looked even more confused. 'How come you gotta sneak back here, ma'am?'

At that moment she heard, across the yard, the sound of the cabin door being violently opened. The voice of her angry husband howled out her name.

'Where in tarnation are you, Betsy?' Applegate bellowed out into the moon-lit yard. 'Betsy? Betsy?'

'Who's that?' Harper wondered.

'That's my husband,' Betsy answered.

'Your what?'

Betsy tossed the canteen to Harper, then gestured to him to remain quiet.

'Don't make a sound, Cy,' she whispered. 'That's my husband and he ain't the understanding kind.'

Harper forced himself up on to one elbow and looked at the terrified young woman.

'What'll he do if he finds me in here?'

She sighed heavily and shook her head.

'There's only one thing I'm sure about, Cy,' she told him. 'If Moses finds you in here he'll fill you with two barrels of buckshot. Don't go fretting, though.'

Harper watched as she wandered out into the yard. He listened as she ushered her husband back into the cabin with a stream of plausible excuses for her being out in the yard in the middle of the night. Harper lay down again and clutched the canteen in his hands.

His dazed mind thought about the beautiful woman who had risked her very life to help him. He then thought about the owner of the deep voice who had bellowed out in the darkness for her to return to the cabin.

'He sure don't sound friendly,' he said to himself with a shudder. 'He don't sound rightly sober, either.'

The stallion moved closer to his prostrate form and lowered its head to snort at the canteen in his hands. Harper raised his hand and patted his mount's neck.

Every nerve in the young drifter's body urged to remain close to the caring Betsy, but something else deep inside him told him that it was best that he should leave. He removed his Stetson and filled its bowl with the water remaining in the canteen. He allowed the stallion to drink his hat dry, then returned it to his head. He slid his fingers into the horse's bridle and gripped it firmly.

'Reckon we'd better head on out of

here, Jet boy,' Harper muttered and once again he gripped a fender and hauled himself to his feet. For a moment he held on to Jet's black mane and shook his weary head. Then he walked unsteadily to the barrel, refilled his canteen and screwed its stopper back on. He made his way back to his mount and hung the vessel from the saddle horn.

'We don't wanna get that gal into any more trouble,' he murmured.

Suddenly his legs gave way beneath him again and he fell to the ground. He rolled over on to his back and stared at his puzzled horse.

Harper shook his head as the severity of his injuries finally dawned on him. He sighed heavily and closed his eyes.

'Maybe we'll stay here for a while longer, Jet.'

7

The desert did not appear quite so dangerous beneath the full moon and multitude of sparkling stars, but that was a delusion. The unholy terrain became no safer when the sun dropped low in the sky to disappear beyond the distant mountains. The lone horseman was well aware of the fact that there was a very good reason for its being known as Satan's Lair. You had to be prepared when you set out for Apache Pass, otherwise you would die. The deadly gunman had no intention of dying.

Lightning Luke Cooper drew rein, stopped his mount beside a tall cactus and stared ahead to where two moonlit shapes lay. Cooper steadied his mount, then tapped his spurs just hard enough to encourage the big horse to trot forwards.

From the cloudless sky moon cast its

eerie illumination across the vast desert around him. He aimed the large black horse directly to where the strange shapes lay. He eased back on his long leathers as he realized what he was looking at.

Two of Brewster's men lay where they had fallen. A dark pool of blood surrounded the corpses and glinted in the moonlight like precious gems.

Lightning Luke dismounted and, keeping a tight hold of his reins, he approached the bodies. The surrounding sand was littered with bullet casings. Cooper leaned down and turned one of the dead men over on to his back. His eyes narrowed at the sight of the pale face.

Cooper removed his gloves and checked both bodies. They were still limp. He straightened up and put his hands back in his gloves thoughtfully.

He could tell that the men had not been dead long. Neither body had been feasted upon by the desert buzzards, so that meant they had been killed after sundown. The more he considered it, the more it looked as though Judge Brewster had something to do with this.

Lightning Luke thought about the telegram he had received, which had promised him a high-paying job in Apache Pass. He led the stallion across the sand to where the ground had been churned up by other horses' hoofs.

The deadly outlaw noted one set of tracks and then another set, made by a larger number of hoofs. It was obvious to Cooper that a solitary rider had been ambushed by several horsemen and had then fled for his life. The two dead men must have belonged to the bushwhackers, he concluded.

Lightning Luke remounted his black stallion. He leaned back against his cantle, pulled out a cigar from his pocket and placed it in the corner of his mouth. He pondered the situation as he struck a match and raised its flame to the tip of his cigar.

As smoke drifted through his lips it

became clearer what exactly had happened. Brewster had tricked him into returning to Apache Pass. The wily old fox had never forgiven Lightning Luke for getting the better of him years back.

Brewster had probably decided that he would collect the reward money on Cooper's head as recompense. The outlaw knew that all the judge and his hired guns had to to do was wait for him to ride his famed black stallion across Satan's Lair and then bushwhack him.

It might have worked if it had been Lightning Luke Cooper who was riding a black stallion across the desert, and not the innocent drifter.

Luckily the young drifter had set out on his own black stallion hours before Cooper had even read the telegram. Brewster and his men had spotted the distinctive horse and just assumed that it was being ridden by Cooper.

Lightning Luke laughed, filled his lungs with cigar smoke and then slowly let it drift through his smiling teeth.

'You made a mistake, Judge,' he hissed. He nodded to himself. It was a mistake the judge would live to regret.

The unknown drifter had unwittingly done him a favour without knowing it, Cooper thought. He had drawn their fire and led them away from their intended target.

The outlaw tapped ash from the end of his cigar and considered what he should do now. Most men would have simply turned the stallion round and headed back to Long Horn City, but not the deadly Cooper. He had something special planned for the judge and his willing henchmen.

Cooper was riled. He had been promised a hefty fee by Brewster and he intended to get it one way or another. His cruel grin grew wider as his merciless mind considered every way he could make the judge pay for his greedy error.

'So you figured on getting your stinking hands on my bounty, huh?' Cooper hissed like a diamond-back rattler as he thought about the judge. 'You reckoned wrong, Judge. All you've managed to do is get my dander up. Now I'm sore. Mighty sore and itching to kill you and your boys.'

The lethal outlaw brooded for a while as he finished his cigar. All of the hoof tracks headed off in the same direction across Satan's Lair to the remote Apache Pass. He knew that Judge Brewster used the settlement as his base of operations.

Lightning Luke tossed the cigar butt down on the sand and nodded to himself again. He knew that once Brewster had discovered his error he would be helpless to do anything other than wait for the real Lightning Luke to arrive in town.

Cooper had travelled this way many times before and knew a dozen short cuts to Apache Pass. He could ride there faster than any of the hired gunmen had ever imagined possible.

'Them back-shooting bastards are gonna get the shock of their lives when they get back to Apache Pass,' he sneered as he checked his arsenal of weapons. 'Nobody double-crosses Lightning Luke and lives.'

He gathered up his long reins and tapped his spurs against the flanks of his mount. The mighty stallion set off at a canter across the sand towards a strange outcrop of rocks lying a little distance away from the hoof marks.

A twisted grin played across the outlaw's lips.

Cooper knew he would reach Apache Pass long before any of them realized that the man they were pursuing was not him. Revenge burned in his heartless soul like a fiery inferno. Nothing could stop him from making the old judge pay the ultimate price. He jabbed his spurs and the black stallion increased its stride. A thousand notions of what he would do to the judge filled Cooper's mind, each one more venomous than the one before.

Judge Brewster was going to pay for his duplicity. Pay with every penny of his ill-gotten fortune and every drop of his blood. The judge would be taught a bitter lesson before meeting his Maker and it was Lightning Luke who was going to teach him.

The outlaw whipped the tails of his long leathers across the powerful shoulders of his horse and thundered through the moonlight towards Apache Pass.

8

Suddenly Cy Harper was awoken from his sleep by a shaft of moonlight which spread over his supine form as the barn door unexpectedly opened. Dragged out of his entangled nightmares and dreams the confused young drifter pulled his six-gun from its holster and trained it nervously at the barn door anxiously. Slowly his eyes focused. The blurred image was unclear but Harper knew who it was.

The sweet-smelling perfume betrayed her.

'Put that gun away,' Betsy's calm voice told him. She closed the door behind her and moved towards him. 'It's only me. I've come to tend that wound of yours.'

Harper returned the gun to its holster and sat upright on the earthen floor. He rubbed the dried sleepy residue from his eyes as she scratched a match and put its flame to a candle. A small area of the barn lit up.

Betsy knelt beside him. As he turned his head he noticed she had brought with her a small tin bowl filled with warm soapy water. A towel was draped over her shoulder and she had a small sewing pouch in the pocket of her dressing-gown.

Harper recalled his plan to leave the farm earlier before he got the handsome young woman into trouble with her husband. He could not remember what had happened or why he was still inside the barn. His confused expression amused Betsy as she pushed a slice of bread and a chunk of cheese into his hand.

'Eat this, Cy,' she instructed. 'It might take that silly expression off your face.'

'What's going on, ma'am?' Harper asked drowsily. Then he realized that she had removed his shirt and was inspecting his torso carefully. He sank his teeth into the cheese and tore off a piece of bread to join it in his mouth.

'I'm gonna sew up this bullet hole, Cy,' she replied firmly, 'before you lose what little blood you've got left. Any objections?'

Before Harper could reply he felt the warm water washing the dirt from the cruel wound with delicate care. It felt good as the soapy suds cleansed his injuries. His eyes darted at her shapely form as she methodically worked at her task. He took another bite of his welcome meal and chewed as he felt the suds trail down his skin. He sighed in a hopeless attempt to ignore the fact that a handsome young woman was so close and bathing him as if he were a baby.

Harper swallowed and then took another bite as he felt his sap rising. He had never chewed so feverishly before.

'I'm not hurting you, am I?' she asked.

He shook his head and kept chewing.

Betsy tilted her head back, blew a strand of her long hair off her face and tucked it behind her ear. Suddenly their eyes met. There was a silence. An embarrassed smile caused Harper to turn his eyes away from her. He sank his teeth into the last of the cheese and then devoured the bread as he tried to think of something else. It was hard. She continued to wash the wound carefully as her cheeks reddened.

'Anything wrong, Cy?' she asked. She could feel her own pulse increasing.

Harper shook his head and swallowed his food as he noticed the splashing water dampen her nightdress. It clung to her seductively. Again he diverted his eyes and stared down at his belt buckle as soapy water dripped into his lap.

Clumsily his hand covered his wet pants.

It was still night but the short sleep had refreshed him more than he would have thought possible. He took deep breaths as she carefully washed his wound. To his surprise it was no longer hurting. It was uncomfortable but the pain that had tormented him was now gone.

Harper glanced at her. He found her sweet smell soothing. He listened to the eerie sounds of night outside the barn and knew that she had risked a lot in returning to him. Then his eyes studied her arms as she worked delicately on him and he saw the bruises. He had not noticed them before but now the candlelight was showing the young drifter every cruel mark on her exposed arms. Harper knew that Betsy's husband enforced his will upon her the hard way.

Harper raised a finger and went to touch the one of the bruises but she pulled back from him. Their eyes met again in silent understanding. He lowered his hand and she continued to wash him like a mother hen tending a wounded chick.

'Did your husband give you them bruises, Betsy?' he asked quietly.

'Ain't none of your business, Cy,' she whispered.

Harper nodded and stared down at his wet pants. He had heard the angry roars of her husband and wondered how he had ever managed to ensnare such a lovely wife. He glanced at her fleetingly.

Who was this kind lady, he wondered. Why would she waste her energies on him?

When she had finished drying his chest she moved quietly behind him and started to sponge his back. He winced as the warm liquid found the torn flesh. He attempted to look over his shoulder at her.

'How come you're tending me, ma'am?' he asked. 'For all you know I'm a no-good outlaw.'

A muffled chuckle spilled from her. 'You need help and I couldn't turn my back on that and I can tell by looking at you that you ain't an outlaw.'

Harper frowned. 'I don't look like I'm wanted?'

Betsy leaned closer to his back. He could feel her breath on his broad shoulders as she spoke.

'You're too sweet to be an outlaw, Cy,' she purred. 'Too young and innocent to be anything except what you are.'

Harper pressed his hands into his lap. 'And what am I?'

'A wounded young critter that needs tending.' Betsy's words brushed over his broad shoulders. 'I'll bet you ain't ever done a mean thing in your whole life.'

He wished that she was correct but he recalled the savagery of the war and what he and so many others had been forced to do in order to survive. His gaze darted up at the rafters, then returned to his lap.

'I did plenty of bad things in the war, Betsy. Real bad and that haunts me,' he admitted. 'I never told anyone that before. I'm ashamed of being alive and that's the truth.'

She dropped the sponge back into the bowl and fell quiet for a few moments. Her hands lifted the towel and she stared at his broad back.

'A lot of folks did bad things in the war, Cy,' she said quietly. 'The thing is, you stopped. Some folks just don't know how to quit doing the bad things they've learned.'

He smiled and nodded. 'You're pretty smart.'

She ruffled his hair in an almost motherly fashion.

'If I was smart I sure wouldn't be stuck here in a loveless marriage, Cy. Nope, I'm not smart.'

'Where's that gruff old husband of yours, ma'am?' Harper enquired as she patted him dry with the towel. 'I don't reckon he'd be too pleased with you tending me like this.'

She did not reply. Betsy just carefully continued to dry the broken skin before placing the towel across his out-stretched legs as he sat like a helpless toddler in front of her.

He watched her expertly thread a needle, then his eyes widened as she moved closer.

'What you gonna do?' he gulped.

Betsy tilted her head and sighed.

'Well I sure ain't gonna start embroidering you with flowers, Cy. You need sewing up so you don't start bleeding again.'

Harper tried to appear unconcerned.

'Oh, yeah. I figured that was what you were intending,' he said.

'You ain't scared, are you?'

He raised his eyebrows. 'I guess I am a little edgy.'

Betsy grinned and pulled him towards her. As the scent of her freshly washed hair filled his nostrils he was lulled into a false sense of security. Then the sharp needle pierced his skin and he gritted his teeth.

'Did I mention that it'll hurt?' she asked, smiling.

He shook his head as she continued to sew the wound in his chest together until it was closed. He stared at her as she brought her lips towards him.

The sleep-starved Harper closed his eyes expectantly and puckered his lips. Then he heard her teeth bite through the cotton. He opened his eyes and watched her as she moved away from him. Betsy looked at him curiously.

'How come you've got that stupid expression on your face?' she asked as she rethreaded the needle.

He raised his eyebrows. 'Damned if I know.'

'Turn around,' she instructed.

Like an obedient puppy, Harper turned around. He could feel her delicate fingers on his back again. She was carefully pulling his ripped skin together to hide the hideous wound of the rifle bullet.

Harper winced but managed to smother the urge to yelp out in pain. He could feel the needle as it penetrated his skin but he could tell that she was doing a good job. He relaxed and glanced at the barn doors.

He wondered what he and Betsy would do if her husband suddenly appeared. She seemed afraid but respectful of her spouse. That was not unusual, he thought. So many women seemed resigned to their fate when it came to unhappy marriages. So many women had lost any chance of finding true love because of the war, and had buried themselves, believing it was their lot to accept whatever hand fate dealt them.

The same religious upbringing had taught Harper that it was not his place to interfere in such matters. But he resolved that if her heavy-handed spouse did appear at the barn door and attempt to beat Betsy again, he would not allow it.

She might belong to another man but that did not mean he could turn a blind eye to any further misdeeds. Just because her husband did not realize what a precious gift he possessed was no excuse.

Betsy methodically pieced his skin together bit by bit as though trying to work out a puzzle. Harper silently envied the brutal man he had never set eyes upon.

'Nearly done, Cy.' Her soft voice

sounded good to the tired young drifter. The feel of her small fingers on his naked back was soothing. The muskiness of her feminine perfume also calmed Harper and reminded him of happier times.

'How'd you end up here?' Harper asked as he felt her tighten the thread. 'By the sound of your accent you're a long way from home.'

'I answered an advertisement in a paper back in New York, Cy.' Betsy sounded amused by her own stupidity. 'I'm what they call a mail-order bride. In other words I'm a pathetic woman who couldn't get herself a man the proper way.'

'We are a tad scarce since the war.'

'I was stupid, Cy.' Betsy sighed. 'Too many dime novels led me to believe things were better out here. My own fault.'

He nodded thoughtfully. 'Don't run yourself down. I guess you had good reason to answer that advertisement.'

She placed both her soft hands on his

shoulders. A thrill of excitement surged through him as he listened to her.

'You see, I always was the romantic type,' she explained. 'I read lots of books about knights in shining armour but they were pretty scarce back home. I had this crazy notion I'd find my true love out here in the West.'

'I'm sorry,' Harper said sympathetically.

Betsy finished her handiwork and rose to her feet. His large hand took her small fingers in his and he stared at the difference between them.

'What you doing, Cy?' Betsy asked him softly.

Harper did not reply. He simply lifted her small hand to his lips and gently kissed each of her fingers in turn before looking into her eyes. The candlelight was dancing in them.

'I'd never hit you, Betsy.'

'I'm a married woman,' she reminded him.

'I know.' He sighed regretfully before releasing her hand.

Betsy emptied the bowl on the floor, gathered the damp towel up and wrapped it around the small pouch with the needle and thread in it. She placed it all in the bowl, then she paused and stared at him. She grinned.

'Another lifetime and I bet you'd have made one hell of a knight in shining armour, Cy,' she said.

He nodded and pointed at his black stallion behind him in the corner of the barn.

'I got me the horse, Betsy. That's a start, ain't it?'

She stood and brushed her fingers through her hair but the long strands would not obey them. They hung seductively over her fresh-faced beauty as she backed away from him. The dampness of her nightdress made it cling to her shapely form like another skin.

'That horse is the wrong colour.' She smiled. 'It's meant to be white.'

He shrugged as he picked up his shirt. 'Reckon so.'

She continued to stare at him as she slowly moved to the barn door and rested her hand upon its flaking surface. She swallowed hard and took a deep breath.

'You rest now, Cy,' she murmured. 'I'll try and sneak some more food in here for you later. Just don't make any noise to attract old Moses.'

He looked at her curiously.

'Moses?' he repeated.

'My husband Moses,' Betsy explained. 'Like I told you, he's mean and he's got himself a double-barrelled shotgun. You be quiet now. Right?'

'Right.' Harper nodded and slid an arm back into his shirtsleeve. When he looked back at the door she was gone again. His head dropped until his chin rested on the knot in his bandanna. Then he caught the scent of her sweet perfume in his flared nostrils. It was overpowering to the wounded young drifter.

It was the fuel of countless dreams.

Dreams that Harper knew could

never come true.

Harper knew that she was right about him.

He was not so naive as suppose that he could remain here with the woman he desired when she had a husband. Some men might have decided to take advantage of the situation but not Cy Harper.

A lifetime had taught him that that would be wrong. When she returned he would be long gone from this place, he vowed. No matter how much he wanted her, Harper knew the only option he had was to leave.

He would face the rifle-toting riders rather than create even more danger for the lovely Betsy.

Harper picked up his hat and placed it on his head. He carefully turned over until his knees were on the ground. He reached out and grabbed his stirrup. He pulled himself up until he was standing. Jet swung his head around and looked at its master. The young man patted the horse's neck.

'We'll head on out,' he whispered to his horse and then paused as his thoughts pondered on Betsy's ultimate fate. 'It's for the best, Jet.'

But no matter how many times he told himself that it was better that they should leave, not one sinew of his tall frame believed it. As he led the stallion to the barn doors he glanced at the sturdy shire horses standing silently in the corner like giants.

Harper mounted the stallion. He touched his hat brim to the watchful horses, then gently encouraged his mount out into the moonlight.

9

As the night progressed along its inevitable path towards the coming of sunrise it grew colder in the desert. Frost now covered the moonlit sand and sparkled like millions of discarded diamonds before the intrepid horseman. The bounty hunter Mort Dooley steered his three horses deeper and deeper into the deadly land known ominously as Satan's Lair. This was no place for the unwary to travel, for it took no prisoners. The bleached bones that littered the desert were testament to that yet the large horseman forged on.

He had the scent of his valuable quarry in his wide nostrils and was not going to turn back now. His only thought was how he was going to spend the small fortune his merciless guns would earn him when the job was done.

There was no doubt in Mort Dooley's mind that he was going to kill Lightning Luke Cooper. When it came to hunting down wanted men or navigating a safe route across arid terrain he had few equals. The notorious bounty hunter had left Long Horn City with two spare saddle mounts in tow. He was taking no chances when it came to crossing Satan's Lair at pace.

The mount beneath him had never before run so quickly for so long, and by the time Dooley reached the spot where the two hired gunmen lay the horse was covered in a thick layer of sweat suds.

The horse had laboured under the weight of the bounty hunter and his arsenal of lethal weapons until it was on the verge of collapse. Dooley kept enough hardware strapped to his saddle to fit out a small army. He was always prepared for whatever his adversaries threw at him.

Dooley hauled back on his reins and stopped the spent horse before it dropped from exhaustion. He eyed the two bodies stretched out on the moonlit sand before him with cold, calculating eyes. He dismounted and led all three horses to where the dead men lay.

His eyes darted around the barren scenery. Whoever had done this was nowhere to be seen or heard. He returned his attention to the bodies.

They appeared inhuman in the eerie moonlight. Their twisted forms were frozen like startled statues upon the sand. Twisted in agony for eternity or until the buzzards tore the flesh from their bones.

Dooley wondered who had killed them. This did not look like the work of Lightning Luke Cooper to the man who hunted outlaws for a living.

His cruel stare surveyed the entire area in search of answers. Dooley knelt between the bodies and scratched a match across his belt buckle. He cupped the flame of the match and held it close to their frozen expressions.

Dooley shook his head and stood up.

He was no wiser. If either man was wanted, the bounty hunter did not recognize their faces. Again his eyes searched the horizon and he saw a couple of saddle horses off in the distance. Dooley reasoned that they belonged to the dead men at his feet.

'What went on here?' he mumbled.

He strode powerfully to the exhausted horse, lifted the fender and hooked its stirrup on to the saddle horn as he released the cinch strap.

He slid the saddle off the horse's back from which a cloud of steam rose up. Dooley walked to one of the other horses. He swung the hefty saddle over the high-shouldered animal's back and reached under its belly to grab the dangling cinch strap. When the saddle was in place Dooley began replacing the leather attachments and the rifles.

It was a job the bounty hunter had repeated many times over his years of chasing wanted men. Within a very few minutes of his arrival at the site of the two bodies he had stripped one horse of its livery and saddled the other.

The bounty hunter gave a last tug on the cinch to satisfy himself that the saddle would not slip. Then he looped his long leathers around the saddle horn and mounted the fresh horse.

Dooley looked around the desert and noted the many hoof tracks that churned up the otherwise virginal sand close to where the bodies had fallen. Then, as he steadied the spirited horse his attention was drawn to another set of tracks.

They were very different from those he had already examined.

These hoof tracks headed in an entirely different direction from all of the others and the bounty hunter wondered why. It then dawned on Dooley that the solitary tracks must have been left by the man he was hunting.

There could be no other explanation.

Dooley knew that the last man to head out from Long Horn was Lightning Luke Cooper. They had to be the tracks of his black stallion, he told himself confidently.

Cooper must have come across the bodies and the disturbed sand just as he, Dooley, had done. Then Lightning Luke had headed off in a different direction from the others.

The question that burned into Dooley's mind was: why? Why would Lightning Luke take a different course?

Dooley knew that, just like himself, the wanted outlaw never took chances. If he had ridden that way there must be a trail that he knew of.

Satan's Lair was not a place for anyone to take risks in crossing. For some reason Cooper had to be heading to Apache Pass by a route that only he knew of.

The bounty hunter released his grip on his exhausted horse and watched the tired animal wander away. He then secured the long leathers of his last spare mount around his saddle horn.

The fearsome looking hunter of two-legged prey considered his options carefully. He could follow the herd or he could trail the lone rider.

It was a simple choice.

If Lightning Luke was headed that way then so was he.

Mort Dooley rammed his bloody spurs into the horse beneath him and forced the wide-eyed animal to start following the solitary set of hoof tracks.

He would get the horse galloping and keep it galloping for as long as necessary. That was how he was always able to catch up with the outlaws he hunted. Dooley refused to quit and rest like normal men. He showed no mercy. Whether it was man or beast, it mattered little to the determined hunter. He just kept riding.

When the mount beneath him was spent he would simply saddle another and repeat the action. Dooley would discard his exhausted horses the way most men throw cigar butts away. He had only one thought on his mind: to catch and kill the men he hunted.

The bounty hunter stared with

narrowed eyes at the moonlit sand and the hoofmarks ahead of him. They stood out in the frosted sand. Dooley knew that he had to catch and kill the legendary Cooper before anyone else got the notion.

Lightning Luke would make him a rich man.

Dooley followed the tracks with renewed determination. The smell of the reward money filled his flared nostrils. He was gaining on the infamous outlaw with every stride of his horse.

This had to be the short cut to the lawless Apache Pass known to only a few, Dooley thought. Lightning Luke Cooper was one of the few.

The bounty hunter spurred on.

10

Apache Pass glowed like a myriad fireflies. Storefronts and street lanterns cast their amber lights across its streets for most of the hours of darkness. It seemed that the town came to life after the blistering sun had set. It could be spotted from miles away even on the darkest of nights but the bright moon in the cloudless sky further illuminated its appearance in an otherwise barren landscape. The intrepid outlaw steered his black mount towards it.

Trees lined the route of the creek but the land beyond them was rocky and as dry as the sand that covered the ground.

Lightning Luke Cooper gazed upon Apache Pass like an eagle considering its next meal. A plan had fomented inside his mind on his journey to the remote town: a plan that would paint the sand red with the blood of his enemies.

The black stallion moved almost silently between the trees that fringed the sprawling settlement, its master peering intently ahead as he approached his destination.

★   ★   ★

Lightning Luke Cooper had made good time from Long Horn City, using his knowledge of the little-known short cut to Apache Pass. It was a route he had taken many times when he needed to travel unseen into the town.

He drew rein beside a sturdy tree and rested a gloved hand against its trunk. He cast his attention along the winding creek to the bright lights of his destination.

The sound of the town's many saloons rang out in the night air. Lightning Luke Cooper wondered whether he would find the men he was pursuing amongst them. He knew that they had headed back to Apache Pass.

He had concluded, after examining the hoof tracks in the desert outside Long Horn City, that there would now be about ten of them. Judge Brewster, it seemed, had been taking no chances. Including the now dead men, there must have been a dozen or more hired gunmen with Brewster when they had opened up on the innocent horseman. That such a number of men were in Brewster's employ told the outlaw how greatly the judge was feared.

He glanced around among the shadows that were shielding him from unwelcome eyes. There was still no sign of the horsemen.

'They'll get one hell of a surprise when they return,' he vowed. Cooper pulled his Winchester from its scabbard and quickly checked that it was fully loaded before returning it back to its leather sheath under his saddle fender.

He drew each of his six-shooters in turn and made sure the desert sand had not found its way into the mechanism of his prized weapons. He blew trail dust off the Peacemakers as his eyes darted around the uninterrupted scene below him. His guns were well oiled and ready to unleash their deathly fury. Cooper holstered his hardware and squinted through the eerie moonlight at the town again. He removed both his gloves and pushed them deep into his coat pockets. He flexed his fingers until they were supple and ready for action.

'Reckon it's time,' he drawled before plucking his canteen off the saddle horn and removing its stopper. He took a long drink. 'I've got a score to settle and a safe to empty.'

Lightning Luke hung the canvas container next to the others and teased the reins to his left. The horse shook its head and then obeyed its silent commands.

The large black stallion walked silently down through the trees and undergrowth towards the east of the settlement as its master continued to look for the man he was determined to teach a valuable lesson.

Before the night was over Brewster would learn that it did not pay to double-cross Lightning Luke Cooper. The stallion crossed the shallow creek and was then guided up behind the buildings.

With every step of the large stallion, its master grew more and more riled. He wanted vengeance for being lured into a bushwhacking. Even though it had failed to achieve its goal, Cooper could never forgive the judge.

A few other witless souls had also tried to betray Lightning Luke in the past. They had all suffered the outlaw's wrath and paid with their lives.

The horse emerged from the shadows of the trees which lined the banks of the creek. It moved at a steady pace into the moonlight that blanketed the town, moonlight which glinted on the barrel of the highly polished six-shooter in Cooper's right hand. The gun rested on the saddle horn as the high shouldered thoroughbred continued on into the town.

Then at the rear of one of the town's many saloons Cooper noticed a man facing a wooden wall. Steam rose from the wall as the man emptied his bladder in inebriated bliss.

The black stallion stopped behind the man, who turned and squinted up at Cooper's lantern-lit features as his shaking hands buttoned his fly.

'Howdy, Luke,' the man greeted him drunkenly. 'Ain't seen you in a month of Sundays. Where you bin, boy?'

Cooper stopped his stallion and stared down at the old-timer as the man staggered to the horse's shoulder.

'Now you ain't seen me, friend,' he corrected. 'I'm not here. Do you savvy?'

The old-timer looked up at the horseman with a puzzled expression on his wrinkled face.

'Sure I see you, Luke. You're right here.'

Cooper shook his head. 'Think, friend. You don't see me at all. I ain't here.'

The old-timer scratched his head.

'Listen up, Luke. I see you plain as day and when I go back in the saloon I'll bring out a dozen or more of my pals. They'll see you as well.'

'I gave you a chance, old-timer,' Lightning Luke told him. Sighing heavily, he pulled a knife from his boot. With a swift thrust of his hand he thrust its long blade into the old man's neck. The drunken man fell backwards, blood pumping from the brutal gash like a fountain. Cooper stared at the now lifeless old-timer.

'Now I'm sure nobody will know I'm in town, friend,' he growled

Cooper wiped the blade across his pants leg and returned it to its hiding-place in the neck of his boot. There was no hint of emotion in the outlaw as he gathered up his reins and tapped his blood-stained spurs into his mount's flanks. The black stallion moved quickly along behind the row of buildings and into a narrow alleyway. Cooper stared with unblinking eyes towards the main street.

He was as wily as a fox. He knew how to get deep into the heart of even the most dangerous of towns without being noticed. He urged his horse along the alley, which cut between the hardware store and the barber shop into the street.

Apache Pass resonated with the sounds of night. Music rang out from the wide-open doors of the saloons in a cheerful cacophany. Lightning Luke ignored the sounds as he rode to the end of the long street. His cold eyes simply searched for danger.

He tapped his spurs again and urged the stallion across the wide street. The black horse walked into another alley-way, where its master drew rein.

With a few tugs of his long leathers, Cooper turned his mount so that he was facing the brightly lit thoroughfare. He threw his leg over the saddle cantle and swiftly dismounted. The busy street was still full of noise as the outlaw secured his leathers to a downpipe.

Lightning Luke could hear the sound

of strumming guitars and tinny pianos coming from all directions. He took a step and then stared down at the jingle bobs on his spurs.

He had no intention of letting them betray him. He bent down, released his spurs from around his boots, then lifted one of his saddlebags' satchel flaps and dropped them in.

He still gripped his gun as he ventured down the alley towards the bright street. He paused and rested his shoulder against the corner of a building as his experienced eyes studied the moonlit street.

The sparkling frost gave Apache Pass an almost peaceful appearance but nothing could be further from the mayhem that Cooper intended to unleash as soon as the judge appeared.

Brewster would pay with every cent he owned and to the very last drop of his blood. Lightning Luke did not care if the judge arrived back in Apache Pass surrounded by a hundred hired body-guards. They could not protect him from the kind of justice that Cooper was eager to dish out.

The outlaw considered the last time he had been in the small town: a time when he had hired his gun skills to Brewster for a tidy sum. Lightning Luke knew that the self-proclaimed judge had a safe in the courthouse full of his ill-gotten gains. Cooper's bank-robbing knowledge came back to him in every detail as he thought about the bank's feebly secured safe.

A wry smile played across his lips.

'I wonder how much money Brewster has accumulated since I was last here?' he asked himself quietly. He pushed his six-gun back into its holster. 'A tidy sum, I'll wager.'

Lightning Luke moved back to the black stallion and swiftly pulled his Winchester free of its scabbard. He cocked its lever. A spent casing flew over his shoulder as he returned to the corner of the building.

He narrowed his eyes.

The deadly outlaw was looking

straight at the courthouse, which was set midway along the street. It stood opposite two of the busy saloons. It was where Brewster dished out his version of the law and had amassed the small fortune that enabled him to control Apache Pass.

Cooper grinned to himself. Being a notorious bank robber, he knew that the courthouse's security precautions could never stop him breaking into it. Its safe was little better.

The sound of boisterous revelry surrounded Cooper as he rested the gleaming barrel of his rifle on his shoulder and walked towards the weatherworn building.

Lightning Luke plucked a cigar from his coat pocket and placed it in the corner of his mouth. His teeth gripped the six-inch-long length of rolled tobacco while he fumbled for a match, found one and scratched it against an upright he passed.

Smoke trailed over his broad shoulder as he flicked the spent match over the heads of a few saddle horses tethered at a hitching rail.

Cooper watched the saloons with keen eyes, noting the variety of the men who stumbled through their swing doors, heading for their next destination; here were at least three whorehouses dotted along the street, their glowing lanterns draped in red lace.

Lightning Luke walked beneath the porch overhangs on his way to the courthouse at a steady pace. He could smell Brewster's money calling out to him. He would divest the building of every damn cent in its safe before the judge and his hired guns returned.

None of the townsfolk seemed to notice the outlaw in their midst as he strode purposefully towards the courthouse. It was just as well; if anyone showed that they had recognized Cooper as he walked confidently along the street he would have killed them instantly.

Lightning Luke Cooper stroked the

trigger of his repeating rifle with his index finger as the weapon rested on his shoulder. He was ready to kill, and when Brewster and his henchmen showed up, he would prove it.

None of the townsfolk saw the lethal outlaw slip through the shadows into the alleyway at the side of the courthouse. Only cigar smoke hanging in the night air might have given any clue as to where Cooper had gone.

11

It had been more than an hour since Betsy left the wounded Cy Harper in the barn after tending his injuries. She had crept back to her matrimonial bed and slipped in unnoticed beside her snoring husband. She had vainly tried to sleep but she could not free herself from thoughts of the handsome drifter in the barn.

Her mind was full of images of the young man she had befriended and they troubled her. She desired his firm body against her own. She wanted to melt into his young arms and forget the mockery of a marriage that her life had become, but knew that her dream could never be realized. Sweat rolled down her beautiful face and trailed into the folds of her bosom.

How could a married woman harbour such immoral thoughts? All Betsy knew was that she did. She rolled on to her side and then returned to her original position. She tossed uneasily in her bed but no matter how hard she tried, sleep eluded her desperate hunt for it. All she could think about was the wounded young drifter in the barn.

Her slender hands pushed her nightdress down against her thighs as if trying to repel the demons that she felt between her legs.

Eventually she just stared at the crude ceiling above her head and listened to the hoglike sounds coming from the man beside her.

Betsy glanced at Moses. He was making more noise than a locomotive with a full head of steam, she thought. Her eyes rolled as her small hands clenched in fists. Why could he not be twenty years younger, she asked herself. Why did he have to become so violent when he was awake?

Betsy brushed away her tears.

This was all there would ever be. She knew that even though something buried deep in her longing heart prayed for more, this was all she could ever expect.

She sighed and thought about the man she knew only as Cy.

Even the darkness had not concealed his youthful good looks from her. She thought of his muscular shoulders and gulped as she recalled how she had felt as she had soaped his bare back and then dried him.

These were evil thoughts.

Ever since Betsy had been a small child she had been taught that married women were not meant to lust over strangers. It was wrong.

Silently she lowered her feet to the floor and carefully eased her slim body off the bed. Betsy looked at the snoring man who seemed totally unaware of anything except his own drunken dreams.

A sadness washed over her.

Betsy lowered her head and stared down at her nightdress as it clung to her pert breasts. She was still in good shape, she told herself.

Not that it mattered.

Betsy looked at Moses as he rolled over on to his back and gave out a deafening snore that filled the room. With no further thought she walked out of the bedroom and across the kitchen area to the door. She opened it and hurried across the yard to the barn. Her hands pulled the heavy doors open and then Betsy stopped in her tracks. As the moonlight cast its eerie illumination across the interior of the barn she stared at the empty space where the man and his black mount had been.

The drifter was gone.

Betsy walked slowly into the barn and looked at the candle as its flame fought against the chilly breeze. Her eyes darted around the empty void. There was little evidence that the wounded Cy and his large horse had even been inside the barn.

She clutched at her stomach.

It felt as though something had been violently ripped from within her. She spun on her heels and looked around the barn as if two such corporeal creatures might be able to hide from her keen sight.

The pair of shire horses were still in their stalls. They watched her and then snorted and stared fearfully beyond her at the open barn doors.

Betsy looked to see what had scared the large horses. Horror filled her at the sight of her raging husband.

'Something's bin going on here, Betsy,' Moses snarled as he rested one of his hands against the wooden wall. 'What are you playing at, gal?'

Frightened, Betsy stared at her husband.

'Moses? You scared me,' she said, clearing her throat nervously. 'I thought I heard something out here and came out to take a look.'

Even half-asleep Moses was not so easily fooled a second time. He moved towards her with blazing eyes and grabbed her arm. She feared that he might tear it from its socket as he drew her close to him.

'Eyewash,' he growled. 'Someone's bin here.'

'Don't be foolish, Moses,' Betsy bluffed. 'There's no one here. Go back to bed. You're tired.'

'You don't ever call me foolish.' The clubbing blow sent Betsy reeling across the earthen floor into the wall. She blinked hard in an attempt to clear her dazed head. She looked up at the jealous Moses as he paced around the barn in search of the man he sensed had been here.

Then he stopped, looked down at his wife and pointed an accusing finger.

'Who was here, wife?'

'Nobody,' she sobbed.

The pig farmer came hurtling towards his terrified wife. He grabbed her long flowing hair and dragged her back up on to her feet. His eyes burned into hers.

'Liar!' he shouted, and struck her again. 'I can smell him. Who was he? Maybe it was your fancy man from back East. Is that it?'

Fear surged like a tidal wave through her every fibre but Betsy refused to betray the innocent young man she had helped.

'No, you're wrong. I'm telling you that no one has been here, Moses,' she lied.

Moses released his grip and walked back out into the yard. He stopped. He stared down at the muddy ground, then looked at Betsy.

'Then who left these hoof tracks, wife?' he demanded with a snort pointed at the moonlit ground. 'Somebody went in and out of my barn on a horse. Look.'

Betsy made her way fearfully to the side of her angry husband as he pointed at the unmistakable marks of the black stallion's hoofs in the muddy ground. She did not know what to say or do.

'Do you see them, Betsy?' Moses yelled at her. 'That's why you was out here earlier, ain't it? Maybe you've bin having visitors every night when I've bin sleeping.'

For a moment Betsy could not utter a word in reply.

'It's one of them dudes from town, ain't it?' he raged.

'No, Moses,' Betsy cried.

'You're lying.' Moses grabbed her wrist and dragged her towards the house at a furious pace. He almost flung her through the door and followed her like a spurned bull ready to punish its mate.

'What you going to do, Moses?' she asked, trembling.

'I'm gonna get dressed and hitch up my horses to the wagon, wife,' he shouted in reply. His big hands plucked his scattergun off the wall. 'Then I'm gonna head on into Apache Pass and find your lover. Then I'm gonna kill him.'

'You can't do that, Moses.' Betsy's voice was shaking like the rest of her bruised being. 'He was just a wounded drifter, that's all. I just washed and stitched up his wounds. Nothing else.'

Her words refuelled his anger.

'You *washed* him? You ain't nothing but a stinking whore. A cheating whore who deserves to be dragged through Apache Pass and then whipped.'

'Nothing happened, Moses,' Betsy sobbed.

'I'm gonna kill him,' Moses grated. 'Then I might kill you as well.'

His jealous rage swelled inside the pig farmer. Moses rested his rifle against the wall and pulled on his britches. Vengeful thoughts burned like branding-irons into his seething imagination. He glared at his terrified wife.

'Get some clothes on, you tramp,' he spat. 'You're coming with me to town. You're gonna watch as I fill your fancy man with buckshot. If you're real lucky I might not kill you as well, gal.'

12

Knowing that the torch-wielding horse-men might still be somewhere along the creek Cy Harper had taken the dusty trail road that passed just behind the small homestead. Every movement of the black stallion ripped through Harper as it trotted over the rough going, but he valiantly gripped the saddle horn as his now rested mount carried him on.

After some little time Harper realized that on the night air he could smell outhouses in need of lime, which told him that there was a town near by. He was getting closer to what he had once called civilization.

The horse made steady speed as it headed for the glowing amber illumination of Apache Pass. The young drifter managed to straighten up when he too noticed the lights ahead of him.

'I sure hope them riflemen didn't come this way, Jet,' he muttered, gathering up his reins. He stared ahead. 'The last thing I need is to tangle with them varmints again.'

Harper had no way of knowing that the men who had put a bullet in his back were now heading for this same small town. The only difference was that they were following the creek, not the moonlit road.

Oblivious to the danger that was fast approaching Apache Pass from a different direction, Harper entered the outskirts of the town and steered his black stallion down the centre of the wide main street. The saloons were doing good business, he noticed as he rode past them.

His mind raced as he remembered the cruel farmer and his young wife. Although he had left them both a few miles behind him, the drifter could not stop thinking about Betsy and what plight she might be facing. He gritted his teeth.

'I need me a drink,' he sighed.

A cold shiver ran along his backbone. It had nothing to do with the frosty temperature. He shook his head and looked up at a long painted board nailed to a veranda.

'The Rotgut Saloon,' he read.

The name amused him, so he nudged his black stallion towards its door.

Outside the brightly lit saloon Harper eased back on his reins and slowly dismounted. He rested for a while and then looked up at the sound of revelry inside the saloon. The voices of men and women filled his ears as he looped his reins over the hitching rail and tied a knot in the long leathers.

After lifting his hat and running his fingers through his hair, Harper patted the black stallion's neck and stepped up on to the boardwalk. He returned his Stetson to his head and then instinctively touched the stitches in his chest.

The wound was numb.

He flexed the fingers of his left hand and carefully rotated his shoulder. The night air had frozen the painful wound but Harper was still grateful that he was right-handed. He glanced with narrowed eyes into the saloon. Its smoke-filled interior drew him like a moth to a flame. He rested a hand upon the swing doors and was about to enter the Rotgut when a drunken man at least twice Harper's age pushed them apart and staggered out into the night air.

Harper tilted his head and observed the swaying figure.

'You OK, mister?' he asked, still resting a hand on the top of one of the swing doors.

The man took a few faltering steps to the edge of the boardwalk and then grabbed hold of a wooden upright as though to stop the saloon from floating away from him. He did not answer the young drifter, his attention was on the black stallion.

'What in tarnation is you doing here back in Apache Pass, boy?' he slurred, speaking to the horse.

Puzzled, Harper stepped up to the

drunk and turned the man's head towards him. He looked into the watery eyes.

'How come you're talking to my horse, mister?' he asked.

The drunken man blinked hard and squinted at Harper in an effort to take in his words. He looked totally confused.

'That ain't your horse,' he averred with a nod of his head. 'Everybody knows that's Lightning Luke's nag, boy. The only black stallion in the territory.'

Harper raised his eyebrows. 'Lightning Luke the outlaw?'

The man clung on to the wooden upright. 'Yeah, the outlaw. That's his horse. Everyone knows Lightning Luke rides a black stallion.'

'That's my horse, mister,' Harper told him.

The drunk frowned then appeared to notice that Harper was at least six inches taller than himself. He sighed and pushed away from the porch upright. He waved his hand over his head.

'I ain't wasting my time talking to you, sonny,' he slurred. 'You're drunk. That's Luke's horse.'

Harper watched as the man walked unsteadily along the street and disappeared round the corner. He then entered the Rotgut and made his way through the crowd to the bar counter.

No sooner had Harper ordered a cold beer than the street outside began to reverberate with the sound of horses' hoofs pounding into town.

'Looks like the judge and his boys are back,' the bartender observed as he polished a glass vigorously.

Harper looked at the man. 'Where they bin, barkeep?' he asked.

The bartender paused in his polishing.

'They've bin trying to get themselves a big bounty, I'm told,' he relied. 'Must be a mighty valuable outlaw to get Judge Brewster on that nag of his.'

'Somebody like Lightning Luke?' Harper hazarded, looking over the suds of his beer.

The bartender nodded. 'Could be.'

Judge Brewster led those who were left of his hired guns as a foolhardy general might lead his troops. He fronted the riders as they made their way down the wide street towards the courthouse. He raised his arm and slowed his pace as they neared the hitching rails outside his office. All the horsemen were dishevelled after hours vainly spent in search of the man whom they had shot and tracked as far as the winding creek.

Brewster reined in and stopped his mount. He stepped down from his saddle and looped his leathers around the twisted wooden rail. His hired gunmen were soon lined up on either side of him.

'I've got two bottles of rye inside, boys,' the judge told them. 'Reckon we've earned the right to drown our sorrows.'

'Where'd you reckon that bastard went to, Judge?' Lane Brown asked, dispirited. 'We must have looked everywhere along the creek trying to find his carcass.'

'Don't none of you fret about Lightning Luke,' Brewster answered confidently. 'I tell you that he must be deader than any of the *hombres* in Boot Hill by now. We'll go looking for his carcass after sunrise.'

'The judge is right,' Dolby agreed. 'We followed his blood trail all the way to the creek. He must have spilled ten pints of blood. He's just gotta be dead by now.'

Although most of the hired gunmen were grunting in agreement with Brewster and Dolby none of them was truly convinced by the argument. They had searched for hours but had not found any sign of either the black stallion or its notorious master.

The hired gunmen dismounted, secured their reins to the pole and stepped up on to the boardwalk beside the weary judge. Brewster searched his vest pockets and handed a key to Red Farrow.

'Open up and get them lamps lit, Red. We got us some hard drinking to do.'

Farrow took the key, twisted it in the lock and marched into the unlit office. Slowly the dark interior of the courthouse started to glow in the light of its coal-oil lanterns.

'Where do you figure Lightning Luke is, Judge?' Lane Brown asked. He licked a cigarette paper and placed the roll-up in the corner of his mouth. 'I find it kinda troubling that we didn't run across his dead carcass.'

Dolby nodded. 'You'd have thought we'd have found that big black stallion of his, Judge.'

Brewster sighed. 'We will. That stallion is the colour of night. When the sun comes up I bet we'll find it straight away.'

'Hold on there a minute, Judge,' Dan Peters said. He was scratching his whiskered jawline and staring across the street towards the Rotgut saloon. 'Lookee yonder, boys. Ain't that a big black stallion tied up outside the Rotgut?'

They all turned and gazed in amazement at the horse Dan Peters was indicating. It was a black stallion.

Brewster pushed his way through his men and stood beside Peters at the edge of the boardwalk. He looked to where the gunman was pointing.

'That's a black stallion OK,' he muttered. 'What's it doing tied up outside the Rotgut?'

'Lightning must be inside the saloon,' Peters gulped.

Suddenly Farrow came rushing out of the courthouse gabbling like a madman. He grabbed the judge by the shoulders and swung him around to face him. He jabbed his hand in the air, pointing at the courthouse.

'What in tarnation are you blethering about, Red?' Brewster yelled. 'Calm down and talk slow enough for us to savvy what you're saying.'

Farrow swallowed hard and steadied his excitement.

'The safe has bin busted clean open,

Judge. There ain't a red cent left inside the damn thing.'

'*What?*' Brewster's voice screeched out as he turned to run into his office. He stared at the wide-open door of his safe. Just as Farrow had stated, it was empty.

'Lightning Luke,' Dolby murmured fearfully. He cast his eyes back at the black stallion. 'He ain't dead. Whoever was spilling that blood, it sure weren't him.'

Brewster glanced along the line of men. 'I don't know how, but Vince is right. It must have bin Lightning Luke Cooper who bust open my safe.'

'And he's planted his big horse over yonder to tell us he ain't dead, Judge,' Brown added. 'That *hombre* is mocking us.'

Dolby frowned. 'You reckoned he was probably dead, Judge.'

Brewster rubbed his chin. 'Looks like I was wrong. Dead wrong. He's stole my money and he wants us to know that he's close.'

'How come he ain't dead?' Farrow wondered.

Brewster rested a hand on his safe. 'All I know for sure is that he ain't. Somehow that bastard is still alive and kicking, boys.'

'He must have figured you double-crossed him, Judge.' Brown sighed. 'Now he's gonna get even.'

'He can try.' Brewster growled.

Suddenly the office rocked to the deafening reports of rapid gunfire coming from out in the street. Rapid rifle fire came bursting through the open doorway from somewhere across the street.

The interior of the courthouse exploded into choking sawdust as hot lead ripped into everything in its path. Too late they realized that Lightning Luke Cooper had them in his rifle's sights. Brewster stared in horror as he watched blood spurt from those of his henchmen closest to the office doorway.

Confusion grew as plumes of crimson gore splashed across the room one

165

after another his hired gunmen fell into pools of blood. Within seconds half of Brewster's men had fallen victim to Cooper's rifle bullets.

Brewster looked around at the only members of his gang he could see to be still on their feet: Dolby, Brown and Farrow. They dragged their guns free of their holsters and started to return fire. Within seconds the courthouse was filled with the choking mix of gun-smoke, smouldering sawdust and the scent of death.

Bleeding profusely, Dan Peters emerged from the carnage. He staggered out on to the boardwalk and pulled the reins of his horse free of the hitching pole. He ducked under the length of wood and grabbed his saddle horn. He put a boot toe into the stirrup and somehow hoisted his blood-covered frame up and on to his horse.

His triumph was short lived.

The gleaming Winchester barrel spat two shots in quick succession from across the wide street. Both bullets hit their target. Peters shook as the bullets thudded into his back. The horse backed away from the courthouse and its lifeless cargo toppled on to the moonlit sand.

As Dolby and his cohorts gathered around the judge at the sides of the door and fired back at the infamous outlaw, another fusillade of deafening red-hot tapers cut across the street and entered the courthouse. Chunks of wood were torn from the walls around the hapless men. Picture frames shattered and showered slivers of glass over the trapped gunmen and their shocked leader.

'Lightning Luke is picking us off like fish in a barrel, Judge,' Brown said as he desperately reloaded his smoking six-shooter. 'How come he don't just high-tail it out of town? He already stole your money. What's he want?'

'He wants the judge,' Farrow told him and spat at the floor.

Brewster looked at the remnants of his once formidable army and shook his head as another outburst of lead deafened them.

'We're all finished if we don't break out of here and kill that varmint fast, boys,' the judge said. He pulled both his .45s from his gunbelt and cocked their hammers.

'Just how do you figure we're gonna do that, Judge?' Dolby asked. He fanned his gun hammer repeatedly, pressed his back against the wall and shook his spent casings from his gun's chambers. 'We're running out of bullets.'

Brewster eyed his last three men and cocked his hammers.

'We gotta get to the horses, boys,' he snarled. 'It's our only chance. We need our Winchesters.'

'We'll be riddled with lead before we can pull our Winchesters free, Vince,' Red Farrow murmured to Dolby.

Dolby gulped. 'Not if we stay low and use the horses as cover,' he murmured back. 'It's our only chance.'

They all resignedly nodded in agreement.

13

The chilling sound of the gun battle that was being waged in Apache Pass rang out along the dusty trail as Moses Applegate lashed his bullwhip across the shoulders of his team of shire horses. The already inebriated pig farmer lifted up a fresh jug of hard liquor and poured it into his dry mouth.

'Let's go back, Moses,' Betsy urged her husband. 'Can't you hear those gunshots? This is madness. We have to turn back.'

Moses placed the jug on the board between them and slapped her across the face. Betsy rocked but was prevented from falling from their high perch by his large hand. He tugged her towards him and snarled into her hair.

'We ain't turning back,' he slurred viciously. 'We're gonna go meet your fancy man so I can teach him it don't pay to sniff around my woman. Besides, that ain't gunplay. That's just thunder. Nothing but thunder.'

Betsy wiped the blood from her mouth and stared through the moonlight at the bright lights of Apache Pass, which was getting closer as every echoing gunshot rang out.

There was no point in arguing with a jug of cheap liquor and she knew it. Her fingers gripped the edge of the driver's board as she waited for the inevitable.

Her eyes glanced upward at the clear moonlit sky. She swallowed hard and stared ahead as the outskirts of Apache Pass came closer.

There was a storm in progress, sure enough. But Betsy knew it was nothing to do with the heavens. This storm was man-made, and spewing from the gun barrels of men with their feet firmly on the ground.

She silently prayed that Cy was not the target this time.

With the street filled with blinding gunsmoke nobody noticed as Lightning Luke Cooper reached up and took hold of the porch overhang. Within seconds the wanted outlaw had clambered up to the balcony. He paced along its entire length, vainly trying to get a clear shot at the men huddled just inside the courthouse.

Then he spotted the approaching wagon which the drunken Moses Applegate was defiantly steering straight into the heart of town.

The quick-witted outlaw knew exactly what he had to do. An evil smile stretched his hardened features as he ran back to the end of the balcony and threw his leg over the railings. He dropped down on to the hard-packed sand and waited for the flatbed wagon.

★   ★   ★

The sound of gunfire echoed around the Rotgut saloon as Harper finished his beer. The startled and terrified men

171

and women around him bolted for the rear doors. In what seemed like less than no time Harper found that he was alone in the saloon.

During a lull in the gunfire the tall youngster strode quickly across the sawdust-covered boards. Resting his shoulder against the doorframe he watched in stunned awe at bullets criss-crossing the street.

He rubbed his stitches. He dried the beer suds off his mouth with his sleeve and cautiously pushed the swing doors apart. Then he raced to where he had left his Jet tethered to a hitching rail. He dropped on to one knee beside a water trough.

He pulled his gun clear of its holster and continued to watch as the red hot tapers traced across the street from both sides. Then his keen eyes narrowed as he noticed a few extinguished torches lying across the saddlebags of two of the horses outside the courthouse.

'Torches. They must be the damn critters that shot me, Jet,' he told the thoroughbred in a soothing voice. He turned his head looked down the street. He spotted a shining rifle barrel as it fired from just behind a corner. 'So who the hell is that?'

As the youngster gathered his tired wits together he recalled the drunken man he had encountered only a few moments before. Harper looked at his horse.

'That drunk reckoned Jet belonged to a wanted outlaw called Lightning Luke,' he said. He rose up to his full height. 'That must be it. Them varmints in that courthouse figured that they were shooting at Lightning Luke when they put a bullet in me. Now he's turned the tables on them.'

Harper watched in bewilderment as the battle continued to rage less than twenty yards from where he was standing. Even though the drifter had been shot by whoever it was in the building, he could not take sides.

'We'd best try and sneak out of this before we get dragged into something which ain't of our making, Jet boy,' he whispered into the horse's ear. 'This sure ain't our fight.'

He tugged his long leathers free and cautiously led the black stallion into an alley beside the Rotgut saloon. Harper rested his head against the saddle leather. It was cool and felt good. He was about to mount and flee from the mayhem when he heard the sound of an approaching vehicle behind him. Harper tilted his head and looked over his shoulder.

The sight that greeted him shook Harper.

'What the hell?'

Even if he had not recognized Betsy the two unmistakable shire horses would have told him immediately whom he was looking at. Harper turned right round as he saw Moses Applegate. The pig farmer was driving his wagon and drinking from his jug at the same time.

Harper looked through the moonlight at Betsy.

The moonlight could not conceal her bruises from his knowing eyes. Harper clenched his fists in anger, then looked to where Lightning Luke was still firing his repeating rifle at the men inside the courthouse. Suddenly he realized that the flatbed wagon was being steered right into the heart of the brutal battle.

'Oh my God!' he gasped. 'They'll be shot to ribbons.'

He swallowed hard and stared at the beautiful face; its image had remained with him ever since he left the barn. Her face bore evidence of recent punishment. Betsy no longer struggled against the firm hand that held her in check. Harper stared at her helplessly.

Then the ear-splitting sound of fresh gunfire made Harper flinch and turn. His eyes darted to the four men who were suddenly making a break from the judge's bullet-ridden office, using their horses as cover in an attempt to escape from the courthouse. He watched as they threw themselves against the flanks of their horses, then he returned his attention to the wagon as the powerful shires pulled it into the main street.

Harper did not notice Brewster and his henchmen haul their repeating rifles from the saddle scabbards. His main concern was for the young woman who sat unwillingly beside her drunken spouse as he waved his jug around.

They were sitting ducks, he thought.

'What the hell is that old fool doing, bringing that wagon into town?' Harper asked himself as he watched Betsy clinging to the iron hand-trim of the seat. 'What's he playing at?'

A shot narrowly missed Harper's head. The youngster ducked and raised his Colt. He returned fire and then glanced again at the wagon as Moses Applegate defiantly drove past Jet's tail. Betsy glanced down at the drifter; sadly and discreetly she shook her head at him.

The sound of Cooper's Winchester unleashing another shot at the four men crouched behind the horses drew Harper's eyes away from Betsy.

'Is that you, Lightning?' Brewster's voice bellowed from outside the office as the wagon moved between the two opposing factions.

'It sure is, you back-shooting double-crosser,' Cooper yelled back. He brought the wagon to an abrupt halt in the middle of the street. 'You ready to die, old-timer?'

Cy Harper frowned and held on to his smoking gun. He watched Moses Applegate exchange his whiskey jug for his large weapon. The farmer raised his double-barrelled scattergun and drew back on its hammers. He looked at his wife.

'Move one muscle and you're a dead whore,' he slurred.

Harper watched as Betsy desperately looked in every direction for somewhere to hide. There was nowhere safe for the defenceless young woman to take refuge.

Lightning Luke cocked his rifle's mechanism and silently watched the inebiated Moses swaying in the driver's box.

'Which one of you varmints bin sniffing around my woman?' Moses bellowed. He swung the barrels of his scattergun in an arc towards the men huddled behind the tethered horses and the wanted outlaw across the street. 'Show yourself or I'll start shooting anyway.'

Lightning Luke Cooper could not see his targets and that riled the lethal outlaw. He levelled his rifle and trained its long barrel on the elderly Moses.

He fired.

A circle of smoke erupted around the weapon as it spewed a white-hot streak of death. The deafening shot passed within inches of the terrified Betsy, still seated next to her husband, and hit Moses dead centre. The pig farmer was lifted off his seat. He flew off the driver's box and crashed into the hard-packed sand.

Not satisfied with his deadly handi-work Cooper tossed his rifle aside and drew one of his six-shooters. He cocked the gun hammer and fired upwards at the cloudless sky. Then he sent a bullet to inches behind the hoofs of the team of shires.

The noise was enough to spook the sturdy horses. They bolted with their cargo in tow. Betsy was thrown backwards on to the flatbed as the driverless wagon raced down the street away from where the pig farmer lay in a pool of his own blood.

The sound of Betsy's helpless cries rang out along the street. Cy Harper holstered his weapon, grabbed his saddle horn and threw himself up on to his saddle. He swung the stallion round and thundered after the wagon.

As Harper passed between the courthouse and the deadly outlaw Cooper the shooting erupted again in earnest.

Shafts of blazing gunfire lit up the long thoroughfare as Brewster and his henchmen vainly tried to keep Lightning Luke Cooper's bullets at bay. As they cocked and fired their rifles over the backs of their terrified horses they suddenly realized that Cooper had moved across the sparkling frost-covered ground to a far better place.

Now the infamous Lightning Luke had an unobstructed view of his targets. The outlaw quickly reloaded his gun and started walking along the board-walk towards Brewster and his last three men.

Dolby squinted through the gun-smoke and saw Cooper with both his six-shooters drawn. He swung around to level his Winchester at the outlaw, but before he could push the hand-guard down Cooper had squeezed both his triggers.

Brown and Farrow were covered in the crimson gore that exploded from the bullet holes in Dolby as he fell at their feet.

Then Lightning Luke fired his guns again.

Farrow fell on to his knees and watched as Brown collapsed beside him. Brewster went to help Farrow at the exact moment that Cooper finished off the hired gunman with a shot to the head.

Judge Brewster stared in horror as the deadly outlaw came on towards him. The older man straightened up and stared at the two guns in Lightning Luke's hands. Smoke trailed from the barrels of his weaponry.

'I don't wanna fight with you, Lightning,' Brewster shouted.

'Too bad, Judge.' Cooper's thumbs pulled back on his gun hammers, then he fired. Flames lit up the shadows as the judge was knocked off his feet by the impact of the outlaw's bullets.

Cooper holstered his guns, then placed a cigar between his teeth. Satisfied that he had avenged himself on the double-crossing judge he turned round and headed back to where he had left his heavily laden black stallion.

'Now it's time we headed on out,' he drawled to the stallion as he reached for the long leathers. He had yet to grasp them when suddenly he heard the unmistakable sound of a gun being cocked behind him. The outlaw's mind raced as he tried to work out who among his adversaries could still be alive. Lightning Luke believed that he had killed them all.

His eyes darted from shadow to shadow. Slowly he tilted his head in search of the unknown gunman.

'You looking for me, Lightning?' The voice of Mort Dooley drew the outlaw around on his boot leather until he saw the big man standing with one of his deadly six-guns in his hand. Dooley was known throughout the West as someone who would keep on hunting his quarry until he had the reward money in his pocket. 'Thanks for leading me to that pot of gold you got hidden in them saddlebags.'

Cooper grinned. 'Take yourself a walk, stranger.'

'Not until I kill you, Lightning,' Dooley responded.

'Who the hell are you?' Cooper drawled as he squared up to the bounty hunter who had one of his many guns aimed straight at him.

'The name's Dooley,' the big man replied.

Cooper stared at the six-shooter in Dooley's hand. It was aimed straight at his midriff. He tilted his head back and looked at the bounty hunter.

'You wouldn't happen to be Mort Dooley the bounty hunter?'

'Yep.' Dooley nodded.

'Only a yella coward don't give a man a fighting chance, Dooley,' Cooper grunted, flexing his fingers over his gun grips.

Mort Dooley did not argue the point. His index finger squeezed his trigger and sent a bullet into the wanted man. A look of disbelieving shock played across Cooper's face as it dawned on him that the bounty hunter's bullet had been perfectly aimed. He took a step forward and then looked down at the blood spreading across his shirt front.

'You killed me, you bastard!' Lightning Luke croaked and then dropped to his knees. The bounty hunter watched as Cooper crashed on to his face and gave out a rasping exhalation of air. Then Dooley strode across the sand and nodded to himself.

'Right on both counts, Lightning,' he whispered.

Finale

Harper had chased the flatbed wagon from Apache Pass out to the edge of the desert. The two enormous spooked horses had hauled the driverless vehicle for more than a quarter of a mile before the determined young horseman had managed to draw level. As he controlled the stallion beneath him, he looked into the back of the fast-moving wagon, where Betsy was clinging to its sides.

She was being thrown from one side to the other as the spooked horses charged on. Harper knew that he had to stop the wagon before Betsy was tossed out of the flatbed.

As the stallion kept level with the thundering shires, Harper freed his cutting rope from the saddle horn, uncoiled its length and skilfully made a loop. Then he spun it above his head.

The sound of the rope being spun

faster and faster sounded like a buzz-saw as Harper steered his mount dangerously close to the pounding hoofs of the pair of shires.

Harper knew that if he made one mistake now he and Betsy could die.

He unleashed his rope.

The loop floated through the moonlight and encircled one of the shire horses' heads. The drifter dragged back on his reins and stopped the stallion beneath him, at the same time wrapping the rope tail around his saddle horn.

When the lasso tightened the lead horse was jerked backwards. It crashed to the ground between the traces. The wagon had come to an abrupt stop as Harper rode up to the flatbed. For a heart-stopping instant the drifter could not see the wagon's precious cargo.

Then he saw her. She was ruffled and shaking as she stood up and stared at her knight in shining armour. He eased the stallion close to the flatbed.

'Are you OK, Betsy?' There was

fearful concern in his voice as he looked anxiously at her for signs of injury.

She blew a loose strand of her hair off her face and smiled at him.

'I thought I'd never see you again, Cy,' she admitted.

He held out his hands to the dishevelled young woman.

'Get up behind me, Betsy,' he said.

'Is Moses dead, Cy?' she asked as she stepped carefully from the wagon and across on to the saddle. She eased herself up on to his bedroll.

Harper released the rope from his saddle horn and watched as the large shire horse got back up on to its legs. Then he looked over his shoulder at Betsy's face. The fresh bruising that he saw there made him reach up and gently touch her cheek.

'Reckon so, Betsy.' Harper sighed. 'There ain't no heart strong enough to handle a bullet.'

'I guess I'm all alone now, Cy.'

'You're not alone, Betsy,' he murmured.

187

Tearfully Betsy buried her head into his broad shoulders and slid her arms around his waist. As she tightened her grip he knew that he would never let her go.

We do hope that you have enjoyed reading this large print book.

Did you know that all of our titles are available for purchase?

We publish a wide range of high quality large print books including:
Romances, Mysteries, Classics
General Fiction
Non Fiction and Westerns

Special interest titles available in large print are:
The Little Oxford Dictionary
Music Book, Song Book
Hymn Book, Service Book

Also available from us courtesy of Oxford University Press:
Young Readers' Dictionary
(large print edition)
Young Readers' Thesaurus
(large print edition)

For further information or a free brochure, please contact us at:
Ulverscroft Large Print Books Ltd.,
The Green, Bradgate Road, Anstey,
Leicester, LE7 7FU, England.
Tel: (00 44) 0116 236 4325
Fax: (00 44) 0116 234 0205

NOLAN'S LAW

Lee Lejeune

After his mother and father die, and the girl he hopes to marry turns him down, Jude James decides to abandon his rented homestead and ride for the West along with Josh, a young exslave seeking sanctuary. Eventually they fall in with a gang led by Brod Nolan, who claims to rob the rich to feed the poor. But there is more to this than meets the eye — and the two friends find themselves embroiled in a series of bloodcurdling encounters in which they must kill or be killed . . .

PIRATES OF THE DESERT

C. J. Sommers

The locals call the sand dunes of the Arizona Territory southland a white ocean. One man, Barney Shivers, carries the comparison a little further when he orders his men to attack any freight shipping that he does not control, and steal the goods on board. A little old lady, Lolly Amos, contracts her nephew, Captain Parthenon Downs of the Arizona rangers, to fight back. Downs eagerly takes on the challenge — but little does he realize that his decision will draw him into a war against two bands of pirates . . .

THE VIGILANCE MAN

Fenton Sadler

For twelve-year-old Brent Cutler, seeing his father lynched was the most powerful influence on his young life, giving him an abiding and lifelong hatred of injustice in any form. As an adult, he returns to the town where he grew up, as a representative of the District Attorney's office — and finds himself going head to head with the man responsible for the death of his father a decade earlier. There will be hard words and tough actions before Cutler can finally lay the demons of his childhood to rest.